His For A Week:

TORMENTED

EM BROWN

Ben:
I told her I **PUNISH** lies, and she still lied to me.

If she thinks she can deceive me, she's going to find out she's wrong the hard way.

I'm going to make her pay…over and over and over again.

His For A Week:

TORMENTED

CHAPTER ONE

What have I done?

Kimani Taylor had slept deep and dreamless, waking alone to the feel of luxury surrounding her body in the form of silken sheets and a feather bed.

Morning light streamed through floor-to-ceiling windows. Last night she had been too exhausted to appreciate the modern elegance of the bedroom that included a panoramic view of San Francisco's Pacific Heights, plush rugs over gleaming hardwood floors, and a gas fireplace six feet wide opposite the bed.

A part of her wanted to stay snuggled in the bed, but she had work to do. Too many times, thanks to one Benjamin Lee and his killer caresses, she had lost sight of her objective: to expose the Scarlet Auction and its exploitation of the women participating in its program. In doing so, she would become the journalist she was meant to be.

No more messing around with Ben. She wasn't here for sex. Or to be someone's fucktoy. Besides, Ben had given—or maybe *extracted* was a better term—enough orgasms to last the week.

But he expected sex. And not just a vanilla

quickie. If she wanted to get her scoop and put a stop to the dubious operations of the Scarlet Auction, how was she going to accomplish that without having sex?

Deciding that the answer might come to her in the course of the day, she looked about the room for clothes but remembered she had left her things on a sofa in the main room, and Ben had torn the tank top she had worn yesterday.

A shiver went through her as memories of his playroom taunted her, making the warmth churn below her belly.

To quell the sensations, she wrapped a sheet around her nakedness and got out of bed. A clock on the wall indicated it was a few minutes past six. She opened the bedroom door and made her way into the living area.

Ben was outside on the basketball court going through what looked like *tai chi* movements. He wore only sweatpants, and she tried her best not to salivate at the sight of his sleek muscles. They had just the right amount of contour and hardness to them, not too puffy or swollen-looking. Most of the time, he had her too tied up to touch him. She imagined what it would feel like to run her hands over his pecs, his abdomen, his—

As if sensing her gaze on him, Ben turned around. His expression seemed to soften before he came inside. She decided that she liked the look of morning stubble about his jaw.

"Did you sleep well?" he asked.

She nodded. "Beats sleeping on the mattress in Jake's basement."

More like the bed was in an entirely different stratosphere.

His gaze took in the bedsheet she wore, and even though he had seen her fully naked, she couldn't help but blush. It was the intensity of his stare. That wolf-eying-red-riding-hood look.

Remembering her resolve to keep focused, she said, "I thought I would get in a shower before getting dressed, if that's okay with you."

"Sure."

"Thanks." She grabbed her things.

"You won't need the clothes from the thrift shop," he said as he headed into the open kitchen.

Was he going to make her walk around naked the whole time, like Jake required of the other women still at the lakeside cabin? She frowned at the thought, even though she had been plenty naked in front of Ben already. "Why not?"

Opening the black stainless refrigerator, he pulled out eggs and cracked a few into a glass.

"Aren't you afraid of getting salmonella?" she asked as she watched him down the raw eggs.

"The eggs are delivered fresh from a farm in Sonoma County. Their chickens are pasture-raised. The chances of salmonella are low."

"I've heard of cage-free eggs, but what's

pasture-raised?"

"Cage-free doesn't always mean the chickens get to roam in the fresh outdoors. They could still be in a cage, only it's barn-sized. And they could still be fed a corn and soy diet."

"Is that bad?"

"Chickens are omnivores. Like many other birds, they eat bugs."

"Oh. That makes sense, though I never thought of chickens that way. Guess I'll think twice next time I buy eggs with the labels 'cage-free' and 'vegetarian-fed.'"

She tucked the information away. There was a lot about the food industry that could make for compelling stories.

"So how do eggs taste raw?" she asked.

"Best way to find out is to try for yourself."

"You don't like them cooked?"

He cracked an egg into a new glass. "I like them cooked but there are certain benefits in their raw state."

He presented her the glass. She stared into it. The yolk stared back.

"Yogurt and granola is more my thing for breakfast…"

She wondered if he was going to make her drink the raw egg the way he made her drink green tea. To beat him to the punch, she downed the egg. She set the glass down as if she had just thrown back a shot of whiskey.

"That went down so fast, did you get a

chance to taste anything?" he asked.

"Not really, but I don't think I'm missing out."

She saw a grin tug a corner of his mouth.

"So about my clothes," she said, "what's the problem with them?"

"You need better clothes to have breakfast at the Pacific Room."

She did a double take. "I'm coming to your meeting?"

He eyed her carefully. "Any reason you shouldn't come?"

Her pulse quickened. Sam, her mentor and editor at the *San Francisco Tribune,* had said she was in a unique position to provide some insight into Oakland's mayoral race as Gordon Lee, one of the frontrunners, was Ben's uncle. Sam had also been interested in the Oakland waterfront property that the Lee family planned to redevelop.

At first she had shared Sam's excitement at the opportunity, and she had initially requested Sam dig into Benjamin Lee because she was worried about who she had been sold to. But Ben was nothing like Jake Whitehurst, who had initially bid on her at the Scarlet Auction.

And she had gone undercover to expose the Scarlet Auction, not cover the Lee family.

"No answer, pet?"

That last word snapped her from her thoughts. She decided she liked it better than

11

Slut #2, Jake's moniker for her, but she wasn't sold on being "pet."

She evaded his question by asking, "This is a work meeting, right? About the waterfront property in Oakland?"

"Is that a problem?" He poured two glasses of water and pushed one across the counter in her direction. "Drink."

She raised a brow. "No green tea?"

"Water first. Most people don't drink enough water."

She walked over and took the glass. "Is this part of your BDSM thing? You like to micromanage what your subs eat and drink?"

"Not always, but when I choose to, I expect you to obey."

The rebel from her teenage years reared its head, but she was wise enough now to know not to fight the smaller battles. She started to drink the water.

"So who's your meeting with?" she asked between sips.

"The head of the Asian Community Alliance in Oakland. Dawson Chang."

She choked on the water. Of all the people for Ben to be meeting with, did it have to be someone who knew her to be a reporter?

"You okay?" he asked after her coughing fit had settled.

She nodded. "Water went down the wrong pipe."

He was looking at her as if he meant to stare straight through her.

"Is it just you and Dawson Chang?" she asked.

He folded his arms. "Why do you ask?"

"Just curious. It seems rather awkward to bring me to a work meeting. Are you going to pass me off as your assistant or something?"

As much as Sam might have loved for her to be a fly on the wall of a meeting between Benjamin Lee and one of the most influential community leaders in the city, she couldn't risk exposing herself. While Dawson might not remember her from two years ago, when she was a journalism student writing a profile on Carlos De Reyes, the youngest person ever to serve on the city's planning commission and one whom Dawson had mentored, she couldn't take that chance.

"I don't have to pass you off as anything," Ben replied.

"Then how are you going to explain my presence?"

"I don't owe him an explanation."

"But Dawson'll wonder."

He raised a brow. "You're on a first-name basis with him?"

"Well, calling him Mr. Chang sounds rather old-fashioned."

He seemed to buy that. For now.

In researching De Reyes' background, she

had come across an old photo of him with Dawson at a noted hangout for the Communist Party. Carlos had admitted to being in the league during his college days and credited Dawson as the biggest influence in his life. According to Carlos, Dawson could do no wrong. She had later interviewed Dawson about Carlos and asked him if he had been a member of the league as well. Dawson had replied, "No comment." At Carlos' request, she had omitted any mention of the league in her write-up.

"What if he thinks I'm your date—or some call girl you picked up?"

He grinned. "Is that better or worse than being my pet?"

She returned his mocking smile with a scowl. But what if he wasn't joking around? She imagined him commanding her to do something embarrassing—like fetching something in the middle of breakfast. It was one thing to engage in petplay in the relative solitude of a cabin in the boondocks of Northern California, and quite another to bring their master-sub relationship into a public place in the community where she had grown up.

"I think you'd get a lot more done without me tagging along," she said.

"You're not expected to participate in the meeting."

"Then why have me there?"

"Because I feel like bringing you along."

"You don't trust me to hang out by myself?"

He narrowed his eyes. "Are you trying to be a difficult pet?"

"I'm trying to help you out. And truth be told, I don't know that I want to sit in a boring developers' meeting."

"You don't strike me as the kind to bore easily," he said. "You strike me as the curious type."

He was assessing her again. She decided to finish her water to show she wasn't trying to be difficult on purpose. What else could she say to persuade him?

"We don't have time to swing by my place to get clothes that would be appropriate for the Pacific Room," she said, even though it wasn't impossible if they hustled.

"I'll take care of it."

"How?"

"My assistant can grab some things from the store."

"No shop is open at this hour."

He turned to his cellphone, which lay on the counter. "Call Beth."

"Good morning, Ben," came a woman's voice after the second ring. "Your reservation is confirmed for the Pacific Room."

"Thank you. I also need reservations for Ishikawa West tonight and to do some clothes shopping for—"

"But I still owe you for the stuff we bought in

Weaverville," Kimani protested, refusing to have someone who didn't know her tastes shop for her.

Ben looked her over. "Female in her mid-twenties. Five foot six. About a hundred twenty pounds. Thirty-eight, twenty-six, thirty-six. Size eight shoes."

"Thirty-eight, twenty-eight, thirty-eight" she corrected under her breath, miffed that he had ignored her *and* had her measurements down. She gestured for his attention and whispered, "But I don't want—"

"I need the clothes in time—"

"I don't want or need new clothes," she tried again a little louder.

"—for my meeting with Dawson."

"That doesn't leave me much time," Beth replied, sounding much less fazed than Kimani would have expected.

"Shop fast."

"Shop fast?" Kimani echoed after Ben had hung up. "Even if your assistant could find a shop open this early in the morning, I don't need new clothes."

"Beth is very resourceful. She'll be here. With the clothes."

Partially intrigued at how this was possible, Kimani speculated aloud, "I guess Target could be open this early."

"Beth will probably get Monica to open her boutique early."

She frowned. "Boutique?"

"Monica is a family friend and owns a boutique downtown."

Kimani usually didn't shop the type of stores that could afford the rent downtown.

As if guessing her thoughts, he said, "You don't have to pay for the clothes."

It probably shouldn't matter to her if he wanted to buy her clothes, given that he had "bought" *her*, but she wanted to maintain a little of her dignity. "Look, I know you could probably afford to buy the whole boutique and then some, but I'm not a charity case and I'm not looking for handouts or gifts."

"Who said I'm giving the clothes to you?"

"You don't plan on returning clothes that have been worn?"

He had made two cups of green tea as they spoke. "Of course not."

"Then what will happen to them after I'm done—assuming I wear any of them."

"I'll have Beth donate them to Goodwill."

She couldn't complain about that. Putting aside the issues of the clothes, however, she still had to find a way out of the meeting with Dawson Chang.

"I'm sure your assistant has better things to do than to go shopping for me," she stated. "Like I said, I'd much rather skip your business meeting."

"You'd still need clothes. For dinner tonight.

And it's not at a noodle house in Chinatown."

"Doing this Scarlet Auction thing is not something I'd like to broadcast to the world. I'd prefer to keep a low profile during this week, so please don't make me go to this meeting in a public restaurant."

He seemed to take what she said into consideration. To keep him in a better mood, she drank all of her green tea, which surprised her with its crisp aroma. She wasn't much of a tea drinker, but this was easily the best tea she had ever had.

"If you want out of this meeting," Ben said slowly as he eyed her in a way that immediately set her on edge, "you had better ante up."

CHAPTER TWO

Her resistance had returned, which was why Ben pushed. He could see her guard come up in the way her chin lifted, her shoulders straightened and her lips moved. Those lush, fuckable lips. He wanted to reach over, haul her over the counter and ravish her in the kitchen. But he had to settle the source of her resistance. Was it the sex or the meeting with Dawson?

What the bloody fuck am I doing?

He had no business bringing her to such an important meeting in the first place. He never brought dates, let alone expensive call girls, to business meetings.

But he liked having Kimani around. Knowing that he only had a limited number of days with her made him want to maximize their time together.

"What kind of 'ante?'" she asked carefully.

"Go take your shower. I'll let you know afterwards."

She wanted to know now, he could tell, but she grabbed her stuff and retreated down the hall back to the bedroom. He sent a follow-up text to Beth about the clothes, then one to Stephens to pull the contract that Jake would have signed with the Scarlet Auction. Jake had texted Ben last night:

> Need to call in my loaner.
> Turns out I'm not supposed
> to sell my sluts to third
> parties. You'll have to bring
> her back.

Fuck that had been Ben's first thought. But it made sense the Scarlet Auction would want to keep matters to only the parties who had signed agreements with them. Nevertheless, he texted Jake:

> Will let you know.

He was far from being done with Kimani, and he wanted his full week with her. His cock had started stirring when he saw her wrapped in his bedsheets, and was now hard as he recalled the many ways she had spent for him last night. He adjusted himself and contemplated what she should ante up. So many options...

The prospects heated his blood. He had to clear his head or he'd be thinking of Kimani during his meeting with Dawson, so he headed down the hall into the bedroom, where he heard the shower going through the bathroom door.

Walking into the bathroom, he saw her standing beneath the waterfall showerhead.

Shampoo suds inched down different parts of her body. The frameless shower doors weren't frosted, so he saw her clearly. He drank in the sight of her breasts, her belly, the black curls at the base of her pelvis, and the rounded arse. His gaze lingered on her buttocks. So ripe for spanking, flogging and caning. And fucking. He remembered well how they'd sounded when he had pounded her from behind last night.

He shed his sweatpants.

Opening her eyes, she gave a gasp upon seeing him. She stiffened.

He didn't get it. Given how receptive she had been to his attentions, why did he feel like he had to seduce her all over again?

No matter. He was more than up for the challenge.

"I'm just about done," she said, staring at his ready erection. "Then the shower is all yours."

"You in a hurry?" he returned, stepping into the shower with her.

"Don't you have to get ready for your meeting with Dawson?"

"There's time."

He turned her around to inspect her derriere. Her arse had recovered amazingly well, with no evidence of the flogging it had received. He could go harder next time.

"I can skip the conditioner," she murmured.

She was about to take a step away from

him, but he had moved his hand from her shoulder to her throat, which stopped her instantly. He stepped into her, molding his body to her backside. Hot water cascaded between them. It rained over his head when he leaned in toward her.

"You saw the state of my cock," he said into her ear. "A good pet asks what she can do to address it."

Still holding her throat in one hand, he moved his other hand over the smoothness of her belly and down between her thighs.

"Isn't it a little early for..."

"For what?"

"Sex."

He liked the sound of the word falling from her lips.

"You have a problem with sex in the morning?" he inquired, dipping his fingers below her mound.

"I don't want to make you late to your meeting."

"Won't happen." And even if it did, it would be worth it. What the hell was she afraid of?

He caressed her slick folds and felt her shiver against him. Desire flared through his groin.

"Now be a good pet and get yourself wet for me," he instructed.

"Are you sure you don't want to—"

He tightened his hold on her throat, pulling

her head till it met his chest. Water poured down her face. He took a step back so that the shower wasn't right over her.

"Do it," he snapped.

She was trying to arch away from his erection, which exaggerated the heaving of her breasts. "I'm not really in the mood."

"Bullshit."

To prove it, he dipped his fingers into her slit and drew out wetness. He put his fingers to her lips.

She turned her face away. "That's probably left over from last night."

"Then you'll have to work on getting some fresh cunt juice."

She didn't have a response this time, but she wasn't taking any action either.

"Are you keeping me waiting, pet?"

"I thought a break might—"

He turned on the body jets and picked her up by her thighs. Spreading her legs, he positioned her cunt in front of one of the jets fixed to the shower walls. She let out a loud gasp as water blasted her between the thighs.

"Shit!" she squealed.

But he held her in place through her writhing. She strained against him, the back of her head digging into his shoulder as she tried to resist how quickly the water pressure was affecting her.

"Oh, God..." she moaned.

He stepped closer to the jet. Her moans turned into cries at the increased intensity. A minute later, she started convulsing, and a loud scream rose above the steam and water swirling about them. She tried to push away from the jet, but he stood firm, tightening his grip on her thighs, prolonging her climax.

Unable to take any more, she shielded herself with her hands, and only then did her body relax. He allowed her slide from him. She collapsed onto the floor. He shut off the jets, leaving only the waterfall on, before squatting down next to her.

He grasped her chin and lifted her gaze to his. "Maybe next time I tell you to get yourself wet, you won't make me do it for you."

Still recovering from her orgasm, she stared at him half dazed. The other half was a mixture of awe and anger. If he were really wicked, he would take the hand shower to her overly sensitive clit. Instead, he kissed her beneath the fall of water, smothering her lips with his. Once more, seeing her spend had caused his arousal to soar. He devoured her mouth until she needed to catch her breath.

"You wet for me now, pet?"

She hesitated, which made him consider another round with the jets, but then she replied, "Yes, Master."

"Show me."

She reached between her thighs and showed

him fingers glistening with a viscous fluid not water.

"How do you know it's not left over from last night?" he asked.

She dared return a smirk. "Why don't you taste it?"

It was an impertinent response for a sub. But he suddenly wanted nothing more than to do what she asked. Grabbing her hand, he jammed her fingers into his mouth, swirling the taste of her over his tongue. He sucked the digits clean.

"Stay there," he said when he was done.

He stepped out of the shower to grab a condom from one of the drawers. After putting it on, he stepped back in and pulled her to her feet. Pressing her back against the shower wall, he returned to ravaging her mouth with his. His cock wanted in something fierce, but he only ground his pelvis into her for now.

He groped her all over, her body warm and slick to the touch. Her resistance had melted and she returned his kiss, making his head swim. Fuck. He couldn't remember wanting a woman this badly before.

He flipped her around to face the wall and pinned her wrists above her head. He held them in place with one hand while his other reached around her hip to fondle her clit. The way her arse arched into him was enough to make him bust a nut.

Bending down, he slid his cock beneath her rump and speared himself into her heat. The movement thrust her farther into the wall, smashing her breasts. To create space for herself, she pressed away from the wall and backed herself farther onto his cock.

Bloody hell. She felt so hot. So fucking good.

A thousand points of pleasure were dancing on his shaft and penetrating into his core. His ardor could not wait, and he started thrusting deep and hard, lifting her to her toes and slamming her into the shower wall.

"Fuck!" she grunted, writhing between him and the wall.

He wasn't sure if she was trying to avoid getting smushed to the wall or if she was returning his thrusts. Either way, it was driving him crazy. But he forced himself to slow down enough to intensify his fondling of her clit till he had her moaning and trembling. He wanted to feel her come on him.

With his cock, he stroked her cunt, building her arousal. The dual assault made quick work of her orgasm. She wailed and erupted into shudders. Her cunt contracted waves of rapture about him. Unable to resist any longer, he shoved himself as far into her as he could. He was going to go all the way. He pounded into her, smacking her arse with every thrust.

His climax bowled into him with surprising force. He drove himself into her as if his life depended on his being inside her as deep as possible. Cum filled the condom. He didn't stop until he was completely drained.

For a whole minute, his legs shook uncontrollably, but he remained buried inside her, relishing her heat and the ways her body curved into his. The shower rained over his shoulders and down between them. When he had regained his legs, he stepped back, allowing her to come off her toes. He let go of her wrists so that she could peel herself from the wall. He caught her when she stumbled and wrapped his arms about her slick body. He stroked her between the legs, eliciting a groan and a shiver. She slumped against him.

"Did you come for me, pet? Twice?"

"Yes, Master," she murmured.

"Did you ask permission?"

CHAPTER THREE

Seriously? Was that one of his rules? She couldn't think straight.

Kimani thought to move away from him to clear her head and get away from the humidity of the shower still raining down on them. But his arms kept her trapped. Her IQ dropped against the feel of his slick, hard body.

"It's not a drought year, but we shouldn't be using this much water," she remarked.

He squeezed a breast, then started pulling at a nipple. "I asked a question, pet."

"Yes!" she yelped. "I mean, no! I didn't ask permission. I forgot. Sorry."

"What do you think would be an appropriate punishment?"

Her mind whirled. Shit. She had no idea.

"I'll give you time to think about it," he said. "If what you propose is acceptable, I'll take your suggestion. If it's not, we do your proposal *and* what I have in mind."

She sucked in her breath. She hated how he always managed to stick her between a rock and a hard place. This was not a good situation. And it had taken him less than an hour to obliterate her resolve not to fool around with him anymore. She was beginning to think it was impossible. Because he made her come *so good.* Because her body reacted to his every touch before she was even cognizant of what was happening. Hell, he didn't even have to touch her. He just had to *look* at her to produce sensations inside her. Reasoning didn't stand a chance.

"What's considered 'acceptable?'" she asked. With his arms wrapped about her, her body continued to hum. To her surprise, she was ready to go at it again. The climax against the shower jet had been agonizing and amazing all at once. She hadn't thought a second orgasm possible because being slammed against the shower wall hadn't been all that comfortable, but it was as if his ardor had seeped into her; his desire expressed in the force with which he dominated her, fueling her lust. Of course, he was more physically powerful than she, and there was something seductive about that. It spoke to a raw, primal instinct.

"You're a smart woman. You'll figure it out."

"I don't get any guidelines whatsoever? That's not very fair."

"Who said life is fair?" He released her. "Finish up but don't get dressed yet. You can wear the robe on the back of the door. Then wait for me in the playroom."

Her traitorous body mourned the loss of his embrace. He waited in the shower, which could have fit four people comfortably, as she quickly ran conditioner through her hair. She then hurried out and wrapped a decadent, oversized towel about herself. She needed to put distance between her and Ben. Seeing him step under the showerhead, the water streaming down his chiseled body, however, she was tempted to stay and watch.

No. Better to go and take advantage of some alone time to think.

Slipping into the large robe, she left the bathroom. But she didn't want to go into the playroom. Standing in the bedroom, she willed herself to focus. A part of her wanted to take the opportunity to run, escape, far from Ben. The whole thing was far too messed up. She should not be this attached to a potential subject of her story. In fact, her involvement with him took him *out* of the story.

But Sam wanted more info on him, or his uncle rather. Maybe that was okay. Or not. At first, like Sam, she had been excited by the special angle she had been given. But now she didn't feel so good about it. Her original intent was to expose the Scarlet Auction and their suspect practices, prevent other women from falling into Marissa's situation—which she felt Claire was perilously close to doing—and thereby land herself a job at the *Tribune*.

But how could she do that *and* get herself untangled from Ben? The man expected her to come up with her own punishment. Having seen what was in his playroom, she did not want to go through with it.

Maybe just a little bit.

Damn her curiosity.

But it might be so cool.

And it might not. She had no doubt that Ben was as good at inflicting pain as he was at pleasure. She'd had a dose of it already and suspected the forthcoming punishment would be tougher. Better to get the hell out while she could.

But then how was she going to get her story? How was she going to stop Jake? She couldn't just leave Claire in his hands.

Hearing that the shower had stopped, she quickly bolted out of the bedroom, down the hall, and into the playroom. He wouldn't be happy if he found she hadn't followed his command. She looked about the room for the safest spot to sit or stand. She opted for the bed. The wrought-iron spindle bed looked innocuous enough, except it was the complete opposite of the other bed in his place. This one looked like it belonged in a jail cell. It didn't have a box spring, let alone pillows and linen.

Ben entered wearing only a towel around his hips. Kimani closed her mouth to keep herself from drooling. He looked so hot with water still dripping off his hair. Unlike most mixed Asians she knew, his hair was jet black. Thick, shiny and straight, it was completely unlike hers. She wanted to run her fingers through his locks, maybe yank them, hard, to make him gasp the way he made *her* gasp.

Standing in front of her, he reached for the sash of her robe, undid the tie, and pulled it from its loops. She braced herself for being tied up.

"About the punishment," she said, "some guidance would be helpful."

"I'm sure it would," he replied placidly, and began wrapping the sash around her eyes.

She pursed her lips in displeasure. Since meeting him, she oscillated between thinking him a nice guy and an asshole. Right now, he was an asshole.

"What are we doing now?" she asked, worried about the deprivation of sight.

He tied the ends of the sash behind her head. "You're lucky I don't usually require my subs to be silent. But none of them ask as many questions as you do."

"So I'm not the quiet type."

"I can tell."

She felt his thumb at her bottom lip.

"I might require you to be silent," he said softly, "just for the fun of it. Or I could simply gag you. You got a preference?"

"Yes. None of the above."

He chuckled, then pushed his thumb into her mouth. Instinctively, she began to suck it.

"Good pet," he crooned.

She wanted to kick herself for the delight his compliment sparked. It wasn't like she was hard up for praise, so why did she like pleasing him?

He pressed down on her tongue. She sucked harder. Would he make her suck his cock next? She remembered the blow job she had given him at Jake's cabin. She had never had to work so hard before because he'd come like three times without ejaculating. She still couldn't quite wrap her head around a non-ejaculating orgasm.

But he had come normally in the shower. So maybe she might get lucky again. Maybe multiple orgasms weren't the norm for Ben. One would think that a woman would be ecstatic to find a guy who could stay hard like Ben. But it made him capable of so much more...and that made Kimani nervous.

"Don't you have to get ready for your meeting?" she asked after he had withdrawn his thumb.

He pulled her to her feet. "I'll worry about the meeting."

The robe was pushed off her shoulders. He led her a few steps from the bed. Orienting herself, she guessed that she was standing next to the tall metal frame that reminded her of a high-bar from men's gymnastics. Only this frame, if she recalled correctly, had leather cuffs dangling from the center.

She was correct.

He lifted an arm above her head, and a cuff soon encircled her wrist. The same was repeated with her other arm.

She should have escaped when she'd had the chance.

"What—are we starting the punishment?" she asked.

"Shhh. Just enjoy the moment."

How was she supposed to do that blindfolded and locked to a metal frame? She didn't like not knowing what to expect. It was why she didn't read or watch a lot of thrillers. Too much suspense.

"I'd enjoy it a lot more if you clued me in on what's going to happen," she told him.

"You should know it's not as exciting without the element of surprise."

Fuck exciting. She didn't want exciting.

"You want to be at my complete mercy. Right, pet?"

She groaned. His seductive voice made it sound inviting. But, no, she didn't want to be at his complete mercy.

His hand gripped the back of her neck, making her gasp.

"Right, pet?"

"Y-Yes."

"You don't sound convinced."

"What else am I supposed to say?" she retorted.

"Look, I won't punish you for telling the

truth. I *will* punish you for lying."

"Then, no. Or, I'm not sure. I don't know you well enough to be convinced."

"Fair enough."

She felt his hands at the cuffs, perhaps checking them. Then his hands slid down her arms and down her back to her butt. She tried to block the sensations his caresses produced.

"That's it?" she questioned. "You're just going to leave it at that?"

"I am."

His hands withdrew, and she heard him walk away. He wasn't going to try to put her at ease?

"Wait!" she called. "Are you just going to leave me here?"

She heard something being turned on. A vibrator, possibly. Hopefully.

"What's that?" she asked, desperately wishing she could see.

"You'll see."

He was standing before her. She could hear the device close to her. She yelped when it touched her nipple. It was a vibrator of some sort.

His fingers were between her thighs, sliding against her moisture. And then the vibrator replaced his fingers. Almost immediately her body hummed in pleasure.

She heard something like tape being pulled, and then she felt it wrapping about her legs. At first, she was worried it was duct tape, but to her surprise, the material didn't stick to her skin as expected, though it bound her thighs together tightly about the vibrator.

She was excited and worried about that vibrator.

This time she remembered to ask permission. "Am I allowed to come?"

"No."

Shit. Now she wasn't so keen on the vibrator. He had taped it there, which meant he didn't expect to remove it anytime soon. Double shit.

"But you stuck a vibrator to me," she protested.

"I control it with this remote." He demonstrated by adjusting the intensity, and she realized the original setting had been relatively low. "If it looks like you're about to come, I'll back it down."

He demonstrated again by bringing the vibration back down to a gentle hum.

"What if you don't turn it down in time?" she challenged.

"You'll have to hold it. And if you don't, you better think of a damn good punishment for yourself later."

She glared at him through the blindfold.

"Don't give me that look, pet," he warned.

She wanted to snap back, "I'm not your pet!"

As if responding to her thoughts, he nudged

the setting up. She bit back a moan.

"I'll try my best, Master," she muttered.

"Good, pet."

He stepped back to view her from head to toe. Walking over to a dresser, he pulled out a red ball gag with nipple clamps dangling from it.

"Open your mouth," he instructed.

"Why?"

"For the ball gag."

She frowned. "Is that really necessary?"

"No," he replied, "but it'll be a pretty ornament on you."

"But how am I going to say my safety word if I'm gagged?"

"You won't need your safety word."

"How can you be sure?"

"If you can take last night, you can handle this."

He pressed the ball gag to her mouth. She pursed her lips, but then parted them without protest. He stuffed the ball into her mouth and secured the gag about her head, then adjusted the length of the chain linking the gag to the nipple clamps before clipping them to her nipples.

"I've got to prepare for my meeting now," he told her. "Since you opted not to go, you can just hang out here for a while."

She heard his footsteps retreat. The door closed. She was alone with the vibrator.

CHAPTER FOUR

As Ben dressed for his meeting, he kept an eye on his mobile, which had an app that displayed the feed from the video camera in the playroom. He could monitor Kimani this way and see her every squirm. She tugged at the cuffs and tried to wriggle away from the vibrator, but he had taped it securely.

Picking up the remote, he increased the intensity a little. She groaned and pulled harder at the cuffs. A good sub would know to take it, not try to escape her predicament.

After getting dressed in a button-down shirt and slacks, he went into the kitchen to pour himself more water and took a call from the lobbyist hired to provide political consulting on the waterfront development. Beth, an extremely slender woman of middle age, arrived during his call with a load of purchases that required the help of two assistants to bring up.

"You texted that you wanted clothes for a few days," she explained when he had finished his call. "You didn't specify what you did or didn't need."

"You didn't have to clear out Monica's store," he said, alternating his gaze between Beth and checking on Kimani.

"She was happy to give you a variety of items. The hard part was getting this." Beth pulled out a blue and gold Warriors t-shirt with a scoop neck. "I woke Greg up with my call. He opened the store in his pajamas."

"Who's Greg?"

"He's the owner of the sporting goods store at the Ashton property. Good thing we didn't raise his rent when his lease renewed, or he might not have been so accommodating."

Ben looked over the many shopping bags and garment bags. "You certainly delivered."

She smiled. "I have to say it was one of my more fun assignments."

He didn't usually like to involve employees in personal affairs, but he knew Beth could get the job done like no one else. And even though he could tell she would have liked an explanation for the shopping request, she knew better than to ask.

She did, however, glance around, perhaps hoping to spot the person she had shopped for. Ben wasn't about to tell her that the intended recipient was tied up in his playroom with a vibrator jammed between her legs.

"Do you want me to lay everything out?"

"Sure."

He checked on his app to see how Kimani was doing. When Beth was done, he said, "Thank you. That's all I need for now."

If she was disappointed, she hid it. "Are you coming by the office today?"

"Not likely."

She nodded. "I'll only call you if it's an emergency, which there won't be any."

He half expected her to wink at him. She motioned for her two assistants to follow her out the door.

After she'd left, he looked back at the livestream app. Kimani had stopped wriggling and had tensed her body from top to bottom. He reached for the remote on the counter and turned the vibrator down. She sighed in relief. But given what he had in mind, she might prefer to have come against his wishes.

As he finished his glass of water, he watched her struggle to keep her orgasm at bay. Even at a low intensity, the vibrator was having its intended effect.

On him, too. His erection pressed against his clothes. She was so bloody hot with her curvy hips and smooth belly. That ball gag looked marvelous on her, too. He wanted to cancel the meeting with Dawson and spend the day fucking her and making her come a hundred different ways.

When it looked like she was having a tough time again, he went into the playroom. Like a fish on a hook, she wriggled sporadically in one direction, then another. He turned off the vibrator and watched as her brow slowly smoothed, her chest heaving as she drew air in carefully, as if the wrong breath might set off an orgasm. A bit of drool trickled past the ball gag. It was fucking sexy.

Ignoring the warmth flaring in his body, he unwrapped the bondage tape and removed the vibrator. She shivered. He wanted to touch her and feel her wet arousal on his fingers, but he wasn't sure he could stop if he started.

Setting aside the tape and vibrator, he took her ankles and attached each to opposite cuffs at the bottom of the bondage frame, stretching her legs.

Now came the wicked part.

From the dresser, he pulled out a steel chastity belt with rubber trim. This one was adjustable and had cost nearly a thousand dollars, which was nowhere near the twenty thousand dollars someone had paid South African goldsmith Uwe Koetter to create one with pearl and gold.

Ben hadn't used this particular chastity belt on anyone before, and he was excited that Kimani would be breaking it in. He adjusted the crotch strap to match her size. She jumped when he fit the belt over her hips. Unlike many chastity belts, the plates on this one didn't extend over the arse. Instead, the back mimicked a thong with an opening at the anus.

Knowing by now what was happening, she shook her head and made protesting sounds against the ball gag. She struggled but the cuffs held her in place. He locked the belt, then removed the nipple clamps and ball gag. The blindfold came off last.

"Since you won't be coming to the meeting, you get to wear this while I'm gone," he explained as he rubbed the crotch strap. She could grind her pussy against rock and not feel a thing. "Wouldn't want you getting off without me."

Nothing but pure mortification radiated from her eyes "You're leaving me tied here? What if I need to pee?!"

"I'm going to release you. And there are a few holes down here to allow urine to pass through."

"And how am I going to wipe myself?"

"You'll have to drip dry."

She returned a look of disgust. "How long am I to wear this thing?"

"Until I get back."

"When will that be?"

"At least two hours."

She looked crestfallen.

"Change your mind about the meeting?" he asked, not sure if he hoped she would or not. He wanted her company, but he was also excited for her to wear the belt.

"No," she said with surprising resolution. "I'll wear the belt."

"You sure?"

She looked away and grumbled, "Yes, I'm sure."

He undid the cuffs from her ankles and wrist. "You can get dressed now. The clothes are out in the living area."

She stared down at the chastity belt, still in a little bit of shock. "You've had this thing cleaned before, right?"

"Consider yourself special. You're the first one in it."

It looked incredible on her.

"Lucky me," she mumbled as she headed, slightly uncertain in her steps, toward the door.

Unable to resist, he grabbed her and pulled her back to him. Her body slammed into his. He crushed his mouth to hers and cupped a buttock, groped her breasts, caressed the small of her back, then gripped the back of her head, holding her in place as his lips and tongue sought her arousal. She ground her pelvis against him and grunted in frustration. The chastity belt was working.

Abruptly, he let her go. She moaned. Her body seemed confused. He guided her out of the playroom and into the living room.

"Your assistant did some serious shopping," she said, looking at all the offerings. As he expected they would, her eyes lit up upon seeing the Golden State Warriors shirt.

"That's more my style," she said, walking past the haute couture to take the basketball shirt. She put it on. Her breasts were perky enough that she didn't need a bra, though her hardened nipples poked at the fabric. "I could just wear the shorts I have with this."

"Don't let the clothes go to waste," he said. "I'm not sending them back."

She raised a brow at him. "If you didn't want that problem, you shouldn't have bought the clothes."

He could have acknowledged the truth of what she said, but he was the Dom here, so it didn't matter. He stood in front of her and fingered the small heart-shaped padlock. "Maybe you want me to stick some Ben Wa balls in you before we put the chastity belt back on?"

She sucked in her breath. No doubt he was coming across as a prick, but he met her glare with a cool stare, daring her to disobey.

She backed down, looked over the options, probably looking for what would go most comfortably with the chastity belt, and grabbed an athletic skirt.

Bataar arrived just after she had slipped on the skirt.

"I need you to drive me to a meeting," Ben told him, tossing him a set of keys. He turned to Kimani. "Wong is at your disposal."

"Your driver?" she replied.

"You'd said you wanted to get your hair done."

She perked up. "Really?"

"Just don't take the whole day."

Thanks to his undergraduate years at Howard, he knew that getting weaves could easily take eight to nine hours. He remembered waiting for a date because her hair wasn't done yet, falling asleep on her sofa, and waking up two hours later to find she was still getting her hair worked on.

"Wong has a mobile if you need to make a call," he added. "And he can take you to breakfast if you want. Or help yourself to anything in the kitchen."

"Thanks," she said.

Hearing her appreciation made him feel less of an asshole. He wondered how else he could please her. He would have expected a woman to drool over the clothes from Monica's boutique, nothing of which would have a price of less than half a grand, yet Kimani had gravitated to the shirt that probably cost a mere thirty dollars.

"I decided to look into this Jake Whitehurst," said Bataar. "He was suspended for three days his junior year in high school."

"Totally not surprising," Kimani muttered.

Ben wasn't impressed in the least. "You're seriously worried about a suspension from high school? If you're going off school records, you have more to worry about from *me*."

"The kid he was accused of bullying committed suicide," Bataar continued.

"Really?" Kimani moved closer to Bataar.

"Were there any charges?"

"It's not against the law to be an asshole," Ben supplied.

"If it were, I wonder how many years *you'd* get? Fifteen to life?"

Bataar's eyebrows shot up. He suppressed a chuckle by coughing.

Ben gave her a cautionary stare. *Careful, pet, I've got more than a chastity belt up my sleeve.*

She got the message and turned to Bataar. "You find anything else on Jake?"

"Not so far," Bataar answered. "You expecting more?"

"Yes and no. He's not dumb, so he wouldn't be advertising his misdeeds. I could have told you he was a bully, and I've known him all of three days. He's also a racist. Not the kind that parades around with white hoods—"

"Jason is one of his best friends," Ben said.

"His racism is more subtle, but when push comes to shove, his true colors show. He's bad news."

"He's an irresponsible prick with small dick syndrome. That doesn't make him a sociopath."

"Are you defending the guy?"

"I think Bataar has better things to do with his time than investigate a racist asshole."

She shook her head. "I disagree. He's capable of hurting someone."

"What makes you say that?" Bataar asked

Kimani seemed to pick her words carefully. "It's not just what he does, it's how he does it."

"It's hard to know when it's just roleplaying. He happens to be a prick as a Dom, too."

She glanced at Bataar, who didn't blink as he was fully aware of his boss' proclivities.

"I just have a sense," she stated.

"A sense. Like women's intuition?"

She lifted her chin. "Something like that."

"You might get further if you have some evidence. Like a bruise."

She touched her cheek. Because he hadn't been there, Ben couldn't say if Jake had acted out of a violent tendency or overzealousness.

"This Whitehurst guy hit you?" Bataar asked.

She stared at Ben. "Maybe he was just 'roleplaying.'"

Bataar turned to Ben for more elucidation, but Ben just said, "We should get going."

Turning to Kimani, he said, "Be good."

She bristled. "You, too."

He stared at her. Maybe she was being insolent because she didn't like being spoken to like that in front of Bataar.

Sensing the tension, Bataar said, "I'll get the car started."

With Bataar gone, Ben walked over to Kimani. Jake had derided him for making a soft impression, and Ben wondered if the prat might not be right. He allowed Kimani a lot more leeway than he normally gave his subs, though most of his subs didn't have the defiant streak that Kimani had.

But it was also deliberate. He was curious to see her full reaction.

He chuckled to himself, then gripped the back of her neck to pull her to him. "By all means, keep that up, pet. I can't wait to hear what you come up with for your punishment."

CHAPTER FIVE

There was no winning against this guy, Kimani thought to herself. Especially when his every touch created chaos with her nerves. His firm, slightly uncomfortable hold on her neck caused her adrenaline to spike.

His gaze dropped to her mouth and he seemed to contemplate kissing her. She half wished he would. Instead, he released her. Taking out his wallet, he pulled out several hundreds and handed them to her.

"You don't have to use any of it," he said before she could protest. " But how are you going to pay your stylist?"

He had a point. "Thank you. I promise I'll pay you back."

"Of course you will."

His eyes glimmered and she found it difficult to swallow. A monetary payment wasn't what he expected.

Only after he had left was she able to breathe normally. She had looked forward to the opportunity to gather her thoughts without the distraction of Ben, but thanks to the chastity belt, she probably wouldn't be able to keep him out of her mind. Her body still hummed from being brought to the verge of coming, only to have the orgasm denied. And she had done her best to fight it. Now there was no way to get herself off.

With a frustrated grunt, she went into the kitchen and looked around for breakfast options. She found a banana and contemplated what she would do with her free time. She could go see Sam. But not at the *Tribune* offices, if she was getting there via Ben's driver. She could swing by her apartment to get her own clothes. Marissa was visiting her folks down in Southern California, so she wouldn't have to bump into her roommate and explain why she was wearing a designer skirt. Whereas Kimani shopped at TJ Maxx and couldn't tell if something came from Neiman Marcus or JCPenny, Marissa had a nose for all things fashion.

"Miss Montana?" asked Wong, knocking on the door.

She let in the small older man.

"Can I take you somewhere, Miss?"

She almost suggested a coffee shop, but then she remembered the chastity belt. If she had to, she would go without drinking anything for as long as possible. Catching her reflection in the mirror, she decided she would definitely get her hair done first.

"You want an appointment *now*?" Keisha asked over the phone when Kimani called her using Wong's cell.

"I need braids stat. I don't have time to fuss about my hair."

"Girl, I'd love to help you out, but I got an appointment at ten this morning."

Kimani thought about the money Ben had given her. "I'll pay your client a hundred bucks to reschedule her appointment. And I'll double your payment if you can do it in just a few hours."

"Damn, why the hurry?"

"I'm working on something. It's hard to explain. Can you help me?"

"I'll see what I can do."

Twenty minutes later, Kimani was seated in a chair at Keisha's house in Visitacion Valley. Coffee in hand but still dressed in her pajamas, Keisha had recruited her younger sister Tara to help out.

"You want *microbraids* done in just a few hours?" Keisha asked with her hands on her hips.

"Well, whatever you think you can do," Kimani answered.

"You want me to sew in some color?"

"Maybe just a little."

As Keisha and Tara got to work, Kimani thought about the punishment she would suggest. She wanted to say that wearing the chastity belt was punishment enough. She couldn't find a comfortable position to sit. And she dreaded having to go to the bathroom with the thing on.

But Ben wouldn't buy that. He'd want something substantive. Something involving the stuff he had in his playroom. The flogger maybe. Or paddle. He had quite the collection of each. Wooden paddles, leather paddles. Paddles with holes, paddles with textures, and even paddles with hearts. As for the floggers, there were at least two dozen...

"So, who's the guy?"

"What's that?" Kimani asked, flushing at the type of thoughts occupying her mind.

"He must be special. You've never had me add color before," Keisha replied.

Kimani was silent as the words sank in. It was true.

"And paying me double, girl? You get a bonus from work or an early Christmas gift?"

"Something like that."

"Or maybe she got herself a sugar daddy?" Tara teased.

"What? I'd never—"

"You got yourself somebody," Keisha said.

"I don't have anybody."

"You can't fool us. You might be busy, but you're resourceful. You have options. You don't have to get microbraids."

Shit. Keisha was right. She had booked this appointment partially so that she wouldn't have to worry about her hair for the next two months, but also out of vanity. Did she want to look good for Ben?

"It's for business," Kimani explained. "Sort ot. I need this guy for a scoop I'm working on. I gotta keep on his good side."

"Un-hunh. Business. Who you think you foolin'?"

Kimani bit her lip. This was worse than she'd thought. Bad enough that she was screwing around with him. But falling for him? That was ten times worse. It would be disastrous.

There was no potential for them. The guy had bought her for sex. No way could he be relationship material. Not that he would choose her even if he was. Aside from basketball and Stanford, they didn't have much in common. And while she understood that opposites attracted, she believed that there had to be enough common ground for a relationship to succeed in the long term.

"Maybe we can skip the color," Kimani said.

"We're doing color. I already envisioned it," Keisha said.

Since there was no use arguing with Keisha, who was so stubborn she'd give mules a run for their money, Kimani tried to steer the conversation to other subjects, to no avail.

"I don't think he even lives here," she said, trying to put an end to their inquiries. "I'm sure his home is in Hong Kong or Beijing."

"But if business brings him to the Bay

Area," Tara said, "who's to say he can't move?"

"I've known the guy for all of three days. If he moves across the world for someone he's known less than a week, I'd have a problem with that."

"You don't believe in love at first sight?"

"I don't, and even if I did, this is not about love or anything romantic! It's business."

"Un-hunh. 'Business,'" Keisha said again, exchanging a look with Tara. "So if it's not about romance, you looking to get laid?"

Kimani felt her face turn into a furnace.

"I never been with an Asian guy before," Tara mused aloud as she wove a dark gold extension into one of the braids. "They any good?"

"I'm not an expert," Kimani objected to the question. "And I bet just like all other men, some of them are good, some aren't..."

"But...?" Keisha prompted.

It was as if she could read Kimani's mind and see the mind-blowing orgasms Ben had pulled out of her, the times he had made her gush so much she'd thought she had peed.

"Girl, you going to braid my hair or what?" Kimani demanded.

Keisha chuckled and turned to Tara. "I think someone's got the hots bad."

"I do not!" Kimani wanted to reply, feeling like she was back in elementary school with her girlfriends taunting her with the "sitting in a tree, k-i-s-s-i-n-g" chant.

By the time her hair was done, she wondered at the wisdom of having come, but when she saw the finished weave in the mirror, she reconsidered.

"Damn, girl," Keisha whistled. "I just made you the hottest sister around."

Kimani studied the braids, dozens of them, with dark browns and gold woven subtly into them. It was the most amazing weave she had ever had.

"If this guy doesn't jump all over you, there's something wrong with him," Tara agreed.

That's what I'm afraid of, Kimani thought to herself.

Then why'd you get your hair done?

After paying Keisha more than double, Kimani had Wong drive her to a coffee shop near the *San Francisco Tribune's* offices in the South of Market district.

"You do something different with your hair?" Sam asked as they sat down at a table, he with a latte and she with a cup of green tea.

"I got braids," she answered.

"Cool. So I looked into what PACs had been formed recently. And there's one called Oakland Forward: A Coalition of Community Members for Oakland's Future. Sounds nice, right? Well, looking at the donor list, it's almost all developers. I'm going to try to talk to Ezra Rosenstein. He's speaking at a Chamber of

Commerce luncheon today."

She knit her brows. "What do you expect to find?"

"It's against the law for an independent expenditure to communicate with a candidate or his campaign."

"What about the Scarlet Auction? Or Jake Whitehurst? You dig up anything there?"

"Nothing interesting about Whitehurst. His father founded the Whitehurst Agency, and they represent a number of players in the NBA and NFL. Jake graduated *cum laude* from USC and went straight to work for his dad's sports agency."

"That's it?"

"That's it. What did you think I was going to find? A criminal record?"

She thought of the college athlete who had been caught raping a drunk woman outside a party. The judge had sentenced the young man to time served. An uproar had followed from people who'd thought the perpetrator had gotten off easy because he was a student at an elite university.

"I guess not," she sighed.

"Is the guy dangerous?"

"I'm pretty sure he is. Just like the guy who beat up my roommate."

Sam's eyes widened. "Did he hurt someone?"

"It's just the way he treats the woman he bid on, who's really young." Kimani wasn't ready to admit what had happened between her and Jake because she didn't want Sam to pull the plug on the story, which he would if he thought she was in danger.

"Are you up close to all this?"

She nodded. "All of us, four couples total, are staying at a remote lakeside cabin somewhere about an hour from Weaverville. It's Jake's cabin. Or at least his dad's."

"And the women are forced to have sex?"

"No, it's consensual. They get paid."

"What about you? How'd you end up there? You said Benjamin Lee wasn't at the auction."

"I was bid on first by Jake. Ben came along and took me off Jake's hands."

"Why did he do that?"

"He saw I didn't like my situation."

"So he's a good Samaritan?"

Sort of. Would a good Samaritan make her wear a chastity belt for hours? But given that she didn't have to be under Jake's thumb anymore, she would credit Ben as a good Samaritan.

"Yeah," she replied. "I lucked out. But the challenge is going to be getting any of the women to go on record with their experiences. We had to sign these crazy-long nondisclosure agreements, and they didn't give us enough time to read everything, especially the fine print."

"So what's your plan?"

"I gotta go back to the cabin, finish out the

week, and try to get to know these women as best I can."

"When are you going back?"

"I'm not sure. Maybe tonight. Ben hasn't said."

"You hear anything about his meeting?"

She hesitated, but answered, "It's with Dawson Chang, head of the Asian Pacific Community Alliance."

"You did a story on Dawson."

"I did a profile on Carlos De Reyes, a protege of Dawson's."

"Anything else?"

"No, I—shouldn't we focus on the Scarlet Auction?"

"You seemed pretty interested in the Lee family when you first called me."

"Yeah, but I don't think there's anything there after all, whereas I *know for sure* the Scarlet Auction is messed up."

"Well, don't be too hasty. I could use a good scoop before the owners' meeting, and I'll take it from wherever."

She remembered he had suggested the possibility the ownership would shut down the paper.

"Okay," she said. "I'll try my best."

Looking down into her mug, she saw that she had drunk most of the tea without realizing it. Great. She had managed to go through the whole morning without needing to go. How much longer could she last?

"I better jet to make it to the Chamber of Commerce luncheon," said Sam as he got up. "Keep me posted."

After he left, she contemplated what she'd told him. She no longer felt keen about digging into Ben's family, but if there was anything illegal going on, then that truth ought to come out. In any case, she doubted what she had told Sam would amount to anything.

She stood up to leave, but Wong had appeared.

"Mr. Lee is on his way here."

CHAPTER SIX

Ben whirled Kimani's pen over the top of his hand as he sat in the passenger seat of his Porsche, with Bataar driving, and took a call from Stephens, who managed special projects for him. Stephens had access to computer hackers and had sent Ben a copy of the contract Jake had signed with the Scarlet Auction.

Jake was right that any selling, lending or granting of his purchase to a third party required authorization from the Scarlet Auction.

To Ben's surprise, Jake hadn't responded to his text yet about Kimani. If Ben didn't have to worry about Jason, he would spend the rest of the week in the Bay Area and have Kimani all to himself. He wondered how she had gotten along with the chastity belt. She had probably cursed him a good deal.

"Bataar had me do background on Jake Whitehurst," Stephens said. "You want more done on him?"

"No," Ben answered. "You get anything else on Kimani Taylor?"

"I could pull her high school transcript," Stephens joked, because he had looked into her undergraduate and graduate school grades. "I stopped looking into her when Bataar put in his request. You want financials? I've got her FICO score and shit like that. She pays off her credit card every month."

"Did Kimani ever work for the *San Francisco Tribune* in any capacity? As an intern?"

"Not that I can find."

"What about this Sam Green guy? Besides teaching one of her classes at the Berkeley journalism school, do they have any other connections together?"

"I'll dig deeper, but nothing else came up at first."

After ending his call with Stephens, Ben returned to the pen he held. It belonged to Kimani. She had looked upset when she couldn't find it in Jake's cabin. Because it wasn't an ordinary pen. Inside, it had a USB, perhaps doubling as a flash drive.

He could simply stick it into the adapter on his iPad to peruse the contents. The only thing holding him back was a sense of decorum/decency. He shouldn't invade her privacy. But then, he *had*—or Stephens had on his behalf—hacked into her student profiles at Stanford and Berkeley, as well as her documents with the Scarlet Auction. The latter had netted him a most delightful questionnaire listing a variety of BDSM activities ranging from petplay to anal fisting. Kimani had rated all of the activities a "5," which meant she couldn't get enough of it.

Based on the hesitancy she had exhibited at different times, he didn't buy all her answers. But why would she lie?

She had also lied about Sam, trying to pass off the editor of the *Tribune* as a worried female friend, when Stephens had discovered Sam was a married gay man. Ben recalled the conversation he had overhead between Kimani and Sam when she'd borrowed his mobile.

They had talked about his family. About Uncle Gordon.

Fuck decency. There was something off about Kimani.

And when had he ever worried about decency? As a young man who had run with a gang, he had stolen things not because he'd needed whatever crap he stole, but because he could. When a rival gang member tried to harass his younger sister, he had beaten the guy beyond what was necessary. He didn't have to break the prick's arm, but he did.

They weren't the most exemplary years of his life. His father's plan to send him to boarding school in England had worked as intended, for the most part.

He was about to stick the pen into the USB adapter hooked to his iPad when the car pulled up in front of the coffee shop where Wong had parked. Setting aside the pen, Ben hopped out of the car.

"Wong can drive," he said to Bataar.

"Better if I drive," Bataar replied. "I can do my job that way."

"How's that?"

"I can keep an eye on you that way."

"You don't work for my dad anymore. You work for me."

"Sorry, boss. Old habits die hard."

Ben thought about how much he itched to get his hands on Kimani. He would have no qualms mauling her in front of his security detail. Nothing surprised or put off Bataar.

"But I'll let you drive," Ben decided.

Shutting the door, he walked over to where Wong stood in front of the SUV reading the *Sing Tao Daily.*

"Who's she having coffee with?" Ben asked.

"I don't know, Mr. Lee. The man just left."

"What did he look like?"

"Medium height, yellow hair, late forties perhaps."

Ben didn't like hearing that Kimani was meeting with a man, but if he was in his late forties, it wasn't as likely to be a date.

"Bataar is driving the rest of the day."

"Yes, Mr. Lee."

Leaving Wong, Ben walked into the small coffee shop.

Fuck.

Normally he was indifferent to weaves, or

how women's hair looked in general, but Kimani looked *hot.* The color at the bottoms of the braids drew attention, but somehow the tops of the braids, by deferring to her bright eyes and thick lashes, accentuated them.

For a few seconds, he couldn't move. All he could do was drink in the sight of her.

She had just risen from her table and, seeing him, looked both disconcerted and relieved. She walked over to him. "I need to *go*, and I don't want to do it wearing the *thing.*"

He couldn't resist a small grin. The situation reminded him of their drive back from Weaverville when she'd needed to piss. He had required her to masturbate herself so that arousal would supersede nature's call.

"You don't like the belt?" he returned.

"That's a rhetorical question, right?"

"What didn't you like about it?"

She blinked several times. "Everything!"

He took one of her braids in hand. He wanted to think she had gotten the extensions for him. "How often did you think about me?"

She sucked in her breath. "Not that often."

"Then the belt didn't do its job. Maybe I should leave it on till it starts to work."

Her eyes flared. He recognized that look in her eyes. It was the same one she had given him just before he'd acquired her. *Fuck you,* her glare had said then. It said that now.

"Okay, I did think about you a lot," she

relented, "but not in the way that you think."

"No? You're not doing a very good job of convincing me to unlock your belt."

She glanced around when a couple at a nearby coffee table got up. Drawing in a breath, she said in as low a voice as possible, "I thought about you a lot, Master."

"Elaborate."

"I thought about what a nice guy you are for making me wear this thing."

He leaned over and whispered in her ear, "I've already said I punish lies. You don't want to know what I do with sarcasm or a bratty sub."

She shivered. She shifted her weight from one foot to the other. The need to piss must be increasing.

"I am grateful my Master made me wear a chastity belt."

"No, you're not. But I'll allow the fib because it's the right thing for a sub to say. What else?"

"I like how you made me all hot and bothered before you put the belt on."

"Another good fib. Did you try to give yourself an orgasm?"

That last word caught the ear of the young man sitting nearest to where they stood.

Ignoring the guy's look, Ben asked, "Did you, pet?"

Kimani had seen the man turn around as well. She lowered her voice more. "I didn't."

"Call me 'Master.'"

"I didn't, Master."

"Why not?"

"How could I have?"

"Would you have if you could?"

She hesitated, then answered, "Yes, Master."

"Would you like to now?"

"Would I what?"

"Like to give yourself an orgasm."

"I just want to pee right now. Please, Master, may I take off the belt?"

"What would you like to do to show me you're a pet worthy of having the chastity belt removed?"

She squeezed her legs tighter together. "What would Master like?"

What he would like to do couldn't be done here, but he knew what he would settle for. He walked to the cashier to acquire the key for the bathroom. Luckily for Kimani, the bathroom was free. After unlocking the door for her, he followed her in. He unbuttoned then unzipped his trousers.

"You want to do something here?" she cried. "In a public bathroom?"

One of the benefits of being a guy was that they didn't get bothered by things like environment. If needed, men could get it up standing in a pile of shit.

"You never do it in a public place, pet?"

She frowned. "Not in a bathroom."

He pulled out his cock and stroked it. "Then

where?"

"In one of the library study rooms at Stanford."

"Where else?"

"In a parking lot of a grocery store—inside the car, at midnight."

"That it?"

"Yeah."

"Now you get to add coffee shop bathroom to your list."

She groaned.

He held his cock, which he had gotten erect for her. "Come on, pet. After the blow job, you can get the chastity belt off."

She looked at the bathroom floor and grimaced. It didn't look bad to him. He had gotten it on in worse places.

"Come on, pet."

Grudgingly, she knelt down, took his cock and wrapped her mouth over the tip.

Fuck.

He closed his eyes, relishing the magnificence of her mouth, before opening his eyes to imprint the sight of her thick lips wrapped about him in his memory. She took him fast and deep, probably because she needed to piss badly. He could be a true asshole and hold off on coming, even though the pressure of her wet, hot mouth was sending delicious vibrations up his prick and down his legs. But he wanted to save up for her punishment later.

He cupped the back of her head and pushed her a little farther down his length. Not yet adept at deep throating, she started to gag. He pulled her off to allow her to stop coughing before he shoved her back on his cock.

Someone knocked on the door.

"Being used," he called out.

Holy shit.

She was sucking harder, her cheeks caved in from the force. Her tongue scraped the underside of his shaft with every bob of the head. She tried taking him deeper of her own accord. With her right hand, she grabbed his bollocks, tugging them just enough to create discomfort.

Fucking marvelous.

While holding her head so she couldn't retreat, he pistoned his hips. For the most part, she was able to keep up, and yanked his scrotum if he made her gag.

Another knock at the door interrupted his rhythm.

"Piss off!" he returned.

He slammed his hips at Kimani. She squeezed his balls and sucked like she was trying to take his cock off.

He exploded into her mouth, shuddering and bucking, grunting and roaring. She swallowed his cum to prevent it from spilling onto herself or the floor.

"That's it, pet, lick it all off," he said with a

ragged breath as a final violent tremor shot through him.

Closing his eyes, he drew in a deep breath. Fuck, that was bloody good.

"Master?"

After replacing his cock and zipping up, he took out a small key and unlocked the chastity belt. She looked at him, waiting.

"You're not leaving, are you?" she asked.

"Why should I?"

She frowned but sat herself on the toilet. Laying the belt over his shoulder, he watched as she relieved herself. When she was done, she went to wash her hands. He barely waited for her to dry them before grabbing her and pinning her face-forward into the wall with her wrists above her head. Pressing her in place with his body, he released one of her wrists, then reached around and under her skirt.

"How's my pussy?" he murmured against her braids.

His digits slid between her folds, then fondled her clitoris. She moaned.

"What are you doing?" she whispered, using her free hand to push herself away from the wall.

"It's no fun putting on a chastity belt if your pussy isn't dripping wet. And because you gave such great head, I might let you come."

CHAPTER SEVEN

Her body was responding already to his caresses. Would it always? Would she never gain control?

"Seriously?" she half-whimpered. "There are people who need to use this bathroom."

"Are you saying you don't want to come?"

No! I do want to come. Make me come...

"Yes...that's what I'm saying."

He slowed his stroking of her clit, then withdrew altogether. With his body no longer pressed against her, she was able to take a breath, albeit a shaky one. He took the chastity belt off his shoulder. She groaned, not wanting to put that thing back on again. But she didn't have much of a choice. So she lifted the skirt and allowed him to wrap the belt about her and lock it in place.

When they exited, they had to walk past three people waiting in line. Kimani felt her face burning and couldn't wait to get out of the coffee shop. Now she would never be able to look at a coffee shop restroom the same way again.

"Uncle Gordon," Ben said into his cell when they had stepped outside. His face darkened, but his tone was light when he spoke. "Meeting was fine. Just one of several Dawson and I will have."

There was a pause, then Ben said, "If you're in the city, I can easily meet for lunch...I'll be there in fifteen minutes."

As Ben hung up, a Porsche Panamera pulled up.

"What happened to Wong?" she asked when he opened the car door for her.

"I gave him the rest of the day off," Ben answered.

Bataar greeted her as she entered the car and settled onto the buttery leather seat, which she could have enjoyed much better without the chastity belt.

"Maybelle's," Ben told Bataar after sitting down next to her.

She started. "We're going for soul food?"

"It's Uncle Gordon's favorite place in the city."

"Really?"

Maybelle's was located on the edge of the Potrero Hill and Bayview districts. The eatery served a mean sweet potato pie, in addition to succulent ribs and perfectly fried chicken.

"He knows the owner somehow."

"So the meeting didn't go so well?" she ventured.

He glanced at her in surprise. "What do you mean?'

"Your meeting with Dawson. You didn't look

too happy about it."

"I didn't?"

"You didn't, even though you told your uncle it went 'fine.'"

"I didn't want to get into it over the phone."

"What went wrong?"

"He made a request I can't fulfill."

"What kind of request?"

"It's expected that a major development like ours must include a certain amount of community space. Dawson Chang wants a childcare center. That's going to take up too much square footage, and the use doesn't fit the property. He knows that."

"Dawson's a smart guy. Why would he do that?"

Ben looked at her carefully before answering, "I don't think he expects to get it. It's just the starting point for negotiation, but I think it's an unreasonable ask to begin with. I think *he* thinks he can push it because Uncle Gordon is running for mayor."

"Do you know where he wants to end up?"

"He probably wants me to buy him out. Instead of building the childcare center at the waterfront property, we'd be money ahead offering to build it somewhere else."

"Why can't a childcare center be profitable for you? There's great demand for childcare."

"It's not more profitable than condos."

"Do more condos serve a greater good?"

"We're taking a poorly utilized property, increasing its value and contributing to the local economy."

"Would it really hurt the value of the development to have a childcare center? I bet you would make out comfortably either way."

"Are you working for APCA?"

"Just trying to understand where you're coming from. So what are you going to do with his request?"

"We'll meet more, look at options, come to a compromise."

She made a wry grin. "You're capable of compromise?"

"What are you saying, pet?"

"You seem to like everything on your terms."

She risked perturbing him with talk like this, but he seemed amused.

"I do like things on my terms. Lift your skirt."

She glanced over at Bataar, who had made no motion, as if he hadn't heard anything, but he had to have heard.

"Do it," Ben said.

She lifted her skirt to reveal the chastity belt. He put his hand at her crotch and rubbed the belt. Instantly, her mind imagined him stroking her sans the belt between them. He had already aroused her prior to putting the damn thing back on.

How was it she hadn't yet learned to keep

her trap closed around this guy? Inevitably she said something that would come back to bite her in some way.

Not wanting to draw Bataar's attention, she remained silent as Ben tapped the belt. She could feel the faintest of pressure on her private parts.

"Maybelle's, boss," Bataar announced.

She let out a huge sigh of relief. Bataar came around to open the door for her.

After he had driven away to park the car or do whatever he normally did till Ben needed him, she murmured to Ben, "You pull that kind of stuff around Bataar often?"

"He's seen a lot more."

"Don't you think it makes him uncomfortable?"

Ben looked down at her. "I don't think it bothers him. And if it did, I compensate him plenty for his discomfort."

"Just because you can take advantage of someone doesn't mean you should. You can still treat him nice."

He caught her chin in his hand, lifting her face up to his. "I'm not a particularly nice guy, but you've already figured that out, eh, pet?"

After he let her go, they walked into the small establishment sandwiched between a laundromat and a barber shop. Like the restaurant in Chinatown, Maybelle's had crammed enough tables and chairs into its space to risk being a fire hazard. The chairs were all folding chairs, mostly mismatched. But who cared about mismatched chairs when the most amazing aroma of barbecue permeated the air?

"It's about a ten, fifteen-minute wait, hon," a waitress called to her as she set down collard greens before a table of patrons.

Just then, a man in his early fifties entered behind them. He stood nearly a good six inches shorter than Ben and wore thin metal glasses over an easy and friendly countenance.

"Uncle Gordon," Ben greeted.

Unlike the stylish and perfectly tailored suit that Ben sported, Gordon Lee wore a much more modest suit. Kimani tried to match their likeness. Gordon had a rounder face, a kinder expression, and faint wrinkles about the eyes suggesting that he liked to laugh a lot.

"This is...Montana," Ben introduced.

Gordon's handshake was warm and firm, his tone welcoming, as if he were truly pleased to meet her. "Gordon Lee."

"Nice to meet you," she said, already drawn to liking him.

Gordon called to the waitress who had spoken to Ben and Kimani, "Aisha, can you put me down for a table for three?"

"Hey there, Mr. Lee," the waitress replied, flashing him a broad smile. "Table for three, coming up."

She turned to a table of two young men. "Charles, Winston, move your butts."

"No, no," Gordon interjected "We're fine waiting."

"They're done, Mr. Lee. Been doing nothing but warming the chairs these past ten minutes." She glared at the two young men, who promptly paid their bill and rose from the table.

"But you have other patrons in line."

"Ma would never let me live it down if she came to find you waiting for a table."

"You tell Maybelle I refuse to jump the line." He gestured to the patrons who had arrived ahead of them to take the newly vacated table.

Aisha put a hand on her hip. "You making trouble for me, Mr. Lee?"

He spotted a highboy where the patrons had just finished up. "No trouble, Aisha. It's all worked out."

"But you should get to sit, Mr. Lee."

"Sitting around too much makes me feel old."

The waitress gave up, wiped down the highboy and said, "I'll tell Ma you're here."

They stood at the table. Gordon smiled at Kimani. "Have you been here before?"

"Quite a few times," she answered.

"You live here in the city then?"

She hesitated, not remembering what she might have told Ben. "I do. But I don't want to get in the way of your meeting with Ben. You can pretend I'm not here. You must have a lot to talk over."

Gordon waved a dismissive hand. "Just boring stuff. And it's not urgent."

The last thing she wanted was for Gordon to ask a bunch of questions about her, so she said, "But it's probably best to talk about the meeting with Dawson while it's fresh on the mind."

"You work for Ben?"

"I told her about the meeting," Ben supplied.

"You said it went fine. That's pretty vague and could be interpreted as good or bad."

Ben gave his uncle the same information he had given Kimani. Meanwhile, plates of brisket, ribs, sweet potato pie, corn, dinner rolls and collard greens were set before them.

"We do need more childcare," Gordon said. "We don't do enough to support parents and young children. The early years are so important when it comes to health and success later in life. Research shows that kids who attend quality preschools have higher math and reading skills, are better prepared for kindergarten, behave better in class, and are more likely to graduate from high school and go to college."

"I turned out okay."

"You're an exception, not the rule."

Gordon stared intently at Ben, leaving something unsaid. Ben bristled and looked away.

Gordon thought for a moment. "There's

actually a building in Chinatown that would be a great location for a preschool or childcare facility. The owner hasn't made any improvements to the property and is just sitting on it."

"Phillip Ma," Ben acknowledged. "His asking price is ridiculous."

"What else did Dawson want?"

"The usual. Use of local labor for construction and transportation improvements because Chinatown is already impacted by surrounding developments."'

"We've had three pedestrian injuries this quarter."

"I almost told Dawson his childcare center proposal was a non-starter, but I know his support means a lot in the mayoral race."

"You do what you have to do. I was thinking of his support when I asked you to meet with him, but that was selfish of me. I should not be a consideration. You have to act in the best interest of the Lee Corporation."

"You're family, Uncle Gordon."

"I appreciate that, but you know that it wasn't my idea to run for mayor."

Kimani had read in the paper that more moderately liberal politicians and the business community had pushed him to run because the other candidates were considered too radical for them. She kept quiet as she scarfed down the food.

"If I don't win the election, I go back to the life I know, which is a pretty good one."

At that moment, a petite elderly woman approached the table. "Gordon Lee, why aren't you sitting at a table?"

"Because I can stand perfectly well," Gordon replied, giving the woman a hug. "Maybelle, this is my nephew, Ben. And this is his guest, Montana."

Maybelle shook hands with them before returning to Gordon. "You know there's always a table at Maybelle's for you." She turned to Ben and Kimani. "This man saved my life."

"I did nothing of the sort," Gordon insisted.

"Without him, I would have been evicted from my apartment while I was recovering from cancer treatment. The landlord was trying to get rid of his Section 8 tenants. Gordon took us on as clients *pro bono*. Which was good, because I could afford next to nothing. I thought I was going to lose it all: my home, my business."

So that's why he's treated as royalty here. Kimani took in the affection beaming from the proprietress' face as she looked upon the mayoral candidate.

Clearly trying to steer the attention off himself, Gordon said, "Maybelle, how are you doing these days?"

"Thinking to open up a second location. Maybe in Oakland. Wish you could come over here and run for mayor so I could vote for you.

Hope you still come to see me if you get elected mayor of Oakland."

"Nothing would stop me from coming, Maybelle. Your sweet potato pie is too good."

"It's to die for," Kimani added.

"Then I'm sending you all home with an extra helping."

After Maybelle left to chat with another table, Kimani couldn't resist asking Gordon what sort of law he practiced.

"I started out in housing and employment," he answered, "usually discrimination cases."

Ben grinned. "Father said he was an oxymoron: a penniless lawyer. He thought it was a waste of a law degree, doing what you did."

"Your father came from humble beginnings. He should know that not everyone's cut out to be a billionaire businessman."

"I'm sure your work must have been very rewarding," Kimani said to Gordon.

"It is," Gordon acknowledged.

Kimani returned his smile. Shoot. She liked the guy. A lot. The few times she had seen him on television, he hadn't come across as very charismatic or well spoken. His demeanor suggested he was more bureaucrat than politician. But up close and personal, his sincerity and affability radiated.

"I don't want to dwell too much on Dawson," Gordon said, returning to their prior topic, "but you know it's hard to get past the commission without the support of APCA."

"I've been in conversation with all the commissioners. I think we could get the votes. Williams, De Reyes, and O'Conner."

"You're not supposed to tell me that kind of stuff. It's against the Brown Act."

"You have to recuse yourself. You don't count."

"You're counting on De Reyes?" Kimani asked. When Ben fixed his stare on her, she thought perhaps she shouldn't have said anything.

"Why can't I count on him?" Ben inquired.

"He's such a progressive. Doesn't seem like the kind of a guy who would approve an upscale development."

"He's supported plenty of condo and mixed-use developments before."

"But only those that have APCA's support," Gordon said.

"De Reyes is considering a run for Oakland City Council," Ben said. "He's starting to court money interests."

"But to go against Dawson?" Kimani queried, wanting to be helpful because she liked Gordon.

"You know Dawson or De Reyes?" Gordon asked.

"Not really. I know *about* them."

"What is it you do? Are you in politics?"

Ben narrowed his eyes. "Yes, what do you

do, Montana?"

CHAPTER EIGHT

"Nothing that interesting. I'm just an office assistant at the moment," Kimani replied.

She had already told him that on their first day, but Ben wanted to see if she was consistent.

"She's a graduate of Stanford," Ben told his uncle.

"Stanford was where I most wanted to go," Gordon said. "I was waitlisted but didn't get in."

"Their loss," Kimani smiled.

"Well, it's a very competitive school. You should be proud you were accepted. What did you study?"

"Communications. One of those degrees you can apply to many fields of work but doesn't actually increase your odds of getting a job."

"What is it you would like to do?"

Kimani didn't have a ready answer. "I'm open to different possibilities."

"Did you go to graduate school?" Ben asked, deliberately putting her on the spot.

"Um...I thought about it."

"Did you do more than think about it?"

Maybelle returned just then with containers

in plastic bags. "I got your extra helpings of sweet potato pie all wrapped up for all o' you. And, Gordon, no use you trying to pay for your lunch. I owe you more than plates of brisket and corn."

"I'm buying," Ben said.

Maybelle arched a brow. "You refusing my generosity?"

"You are too kind, Maybelle," Gordon said.

After Maybelle left, Gordon left a sixty dollar "tip."

"I should get back to my office," he said. "I'm expecting a call within the hour. It was nice to meet you, Montana."

As Kimani and Ben waited outside for Bataar to pull the car up, she said, "Gordon seems like a great guy."

"He would make a good mayor."

"I can see that."

He opened the door for her. It pleased him that she liked Uncle Gordon, and that she had agreed to come to the lunch. He had expected her to resist, the way she had with the breakfast with Dawson. Maybe the chastity belt had put her in a more submissive frame of mind.

After getting in the car himself, and before she could buckle her seat belt, he yanked her to him and clamped his mouth down on hers. Though lunch had been more than filling, he was hungry for something else.

Cupping her head in hand, he smothered

her lips till she could barely catch her breath. He pushed his tongue into her mouth, tasting the faint aroma of bacon from the collard greens. Over and over, he plunged himself into the depths of her mouth and bit her succulent lips, wondering if he could ever get enough of them.

He pulled her onto his lap and had her sit facing forward, turning her head so he could continue his assault on her mouth.

"Can't you—mm—wait till we—mmph—get back to your place?" she murmured against his lips.

Grabbing both thighs, he spread her legs. He stroked her through the chastity belt. He knew she couldn't feel his hand through the device, but sometimes *thought* could create phantom sensations. Shoving his other hand up her shirt, he palmed a breast. He squeezed the delicious flesh, then pinched the nipple, making her gasp and writhe. Her wriggling caused his groin to tighten.

"You're so fucking hot when you squirm," he muttered.

She stilled, not knowing whether to move or not. He recalled how he had made her come—made her squirt—when he had her in a similar position on one of the lounge chairs at Jake's cabin.

"Incoming call from Rosenstein, boss," Bataar said, ruining the moment.

Ben had received a call during lunch from

Ezra but allowed it to go to voicemail. *This had better be bloody important.*

He released his hold of Kimani, and she scrambled back to her seat. He was about to let the call come in on the car's speaker but decided at the last second to pick it up on his mobile.

"Ezra, I'm in the middle of something," he said, adjusting the tightness at his crotch. He imagined making Kimani suck him off in the back of the car.

"This won't take long. I just thought it was important to let you know that a reporter came up to me after my talk at a Chamber of Commerce lunch. He asked about our PAC."

"It's not *our* committee, remember? Who came up to you?"

"I don't remember his name. Some fellow from the *San Francisco Tribune.*"

Ben looked over at Kimani, who was still a little breathless from his manhandling of her. "What did he want?"

"He asked a lot of questions, how much we had raised, who was on the committee. He wanted to know what your involvement was."

"Why would he think I was involved?"

"I don't know. I swear I haven't mentioned you at all."

"Do you think you could track down his name?"

"I can try. I didn't stay to get his business card. I just wanted out as fast as possible before he asked more questions."

"Get a name and call me back."

After hanging up, Ben told Bataar to drive back to the penthouse. He put a hand into his pocket and fingered Kimani's pen.

"Do you know how Claire is doing?" she asked.

Ben dialed Jason, but his cousin didn't answer. He left a text for Jason to call him back.

"Are we going to head back to the cabin later today or tomorrow?"

"You want to?"

She thought for a moment. "I'd like to."

"Why's that?"

"I feel like I've abandoned the other women."

"They have plenty of company."

"And I left something at in the cabin."

"What's that?"

"My pen. I couldn't find it before we left."

"I have plenty of pens you can help yourself to."

She lowered her lashes. "This one, uh, has sentimental value."

"And you decided to bring something of value along on a week of sex?"

"It's like a good luck charm."

He didn't tell her that her so-called charm was about to run out of luck.

CHAPTER NINE

Something was up. Kimani could sense it. She'd often felt Ben's penetrating gaze on her, but either it was more intense on the drive back to his place or it was more frequent. Or both.

Often in these instances, when she met his stare, she could see lust swimming in his eyes. The dilated pools of black made her heart quicken. But his pupils were more constricted at the moment. She found it difficult to swallow. And when he closed the door of his penthouse behind them, she felt as if he were closing her only escape.

It was just as well. She needed to have her guard up after all that talk with Keisha. At lunch, she had relaxed because of Gordon. Now that she was alone with Ben, she needed to watch herself. She didn't like that he had left her hot and bothered once again. And even though she wouldn't be doing anything differently if she didn't have the chastity belt on, knowing it was there only increased her agitation.

He did it to deliberately frustrate you. To keep you down and assert his dominance. You don't want to fall for a guy like that, do you?

He put the sweet potato pie, his keys, and cell on the kitchen counter before turning to her. Leaning back against the counter, he said, "There something you want to tell me, Kimani?"

Kimani. He had used her name instead of calling her "my pet." Was that good or bad?

"Like what?" she returned.

"Like who you had coffee with this morning."

Was he jealous? That might explain the tenseness she had picked up on.

"Just an old friend," she replied nonchalantly, making sure she stood within leaping distance of the front door.

"How come you didn't meet with Sam?"

She gave him a quizzical look.

"Your girlfriend Sam, who used to be a man, who was so worried about you that you felt the need to call or text her on a daily basis. You had the whole morning to yourself, and you chose to have your hair done and meet with someone other than Sam."

"Oh. Sam doesn't live in the city."

Did he suspect Sam was a boyfriend or lover of hers? She thought he didn't care if she was in a relationship with anyone.

Standing up, he tossed her his cell. "Check your email."

"My email?"

"The lab results should be in."

Oh. That. Yesterday, he'd had a nurse draw

blood. He had not undergone the Scarlet Auction's STD testing. She had already engaged in some risky sexual activity, but he hadn't penetrated her yet without a condom.

On his phone, she navigated to her email service provider and logged in. Near the top of the inbox was an email from a lab. She clicked it and read the message. She wasn't surprised that all the test results were negative, but it was still comforting to have confirmation.

"What does it say?" he asked.

"You're clean," she replied as she logged out before tossing him back his phone.

He took off his suit jacket and hung it over the back of one of the barstools at the kitchen counter. "So how is it an office assistant in a financial firm knows about an Oakland planning commissioner and a Chinatown community leader?"

"My parents live in Oakland. I guess I heard or read about Dawson and Carlos."

Why is he asking so many questions?

"And why are you so convinced De Reyes won't go against ACPA?"

"I understand they're close."

"How close?"

"Close enough that Carlos won't go against Dawson."

He was staring at her with a mixture of the wolf wanting to eat Red Riding Hood and something else. Maybe she should stop talking.

92

She was trying to be helpful but had the feeling she was going to get herself in trouble somehow.

"So you know De Reyes and Chang—excuse me, Carlos and Dawson."

She faked a nonchalant shrug. "I'm sure a lot of people could tell you that Carl—De Reyes and Chang are close."

"Yet no one has. Not even the lobbyist who I'm paying good money for information like that."

"Maybe you should get yourself a new lobbyist."

He had rolled up his sleeves and took a step toward her. "Or maybe I could hire *you*. How about it? You tell me exactly what you know. I'll compensate you what I'm paying the lobbyist. His retainer is twenty thousand a month."

Twenty thousand?! Holy crap.

But there was no way she would divulge what was told to her off the record.

"I don't know that much," she downplayed. "Certainly nothing worth twenty thousand dollars."

"Funny that. Most people try to negotiate the dollar amount *up*."

"I'm keeping it real. I'm not going to scam you, even if I did know anything worth paying for."

"I'm offering twenty thousand dollars. You were hard up enough for money that you got involved with the Scarlet Auction. I doubt you'll see twenty thousand from *them*."

"That's different."

"How so?"

He was closing the distance between them.

"Mind if I help myself to some water?" she asked, trying to skirt around the sofa and head to the relative safety of the kitchen.

But he caught her about the waist and tossed her into the leather armchair. He braced himself against the arms, caging her in. "Suddenly you don't seem to need money so badly."

She narrowed her eyes at him. "Do all rich people think they can just toss around big numbers and expect they can awe us into getting what they want?"

"Okay. How about I offer something else instead?"

He slid his hand up her skirt and along her thigh, making her jump.

"Like I said, I don't know anything."

Dammit. Her words had come out shaky.

He leaned in closer. "That's a lie, Kimani. Do you remember what I do with lies?"

CHAPTER TEN

Ben stared at Kimani, warmth stirring in his abdomen despite his present vexation with her. She was a good liar but not a perfect one. What were the chances that the *Tribune* reporter who had approached Ezra was her Sam? And was Sam whom she had met with at the coffee shop? He was ready for answers, and he was going to get them one way or another.

Scooping her up, he threw her over his shoulder and stalked into his playroom.

"What the—what are you doing?" she asked, trying to wriggle off him as if she had somewhere to go.

Once inside the playroom, he set her down. "You like to rack up the punishments, don't you, pet?"

She tried to brush past by him to get to the door.

"Now is that the way for a good pet to behave?" he asked, thrusting her from the door. He wasn't usually this obstinate, but he'd never had a sub try to escape before.

"False imprisonment is a felony," she threatened.

He raised his brows but decided to call her on her threat. He stepped away from the door, allowing her access. "Go ahead. But if you decide to come back, your punishment is doubled."

She stared at the door.

To his surprise, he grew uneasy about his gamble. His pulse quickened, and he wondered if he ought to have provided her an out so soon. He didn't want her to leave, but he suspected she had reasons to stay.

Turning her head, she glared at him. "You know, I was just trying to be helpful. There's no need to make a mountain out of a molehill."

He felt relief. She wasn't leaving. But that didn't mean he wasn't going to go through with his punishment.

"I'm the one making a mountain?" he returned. "There a reason you won't just tell me what you know?"

She returned his stare in silence. He could see her thoughts churning.

"Right," he muttered to himself.

Stepping to her, he whipped the shirt over her head and pulled it down her arms, stopping at the wrists. Her baps bounced enticingly at him. He twisted the shirt into a knot, locking her wrists together.

She gasped. "Ow! That's tight!"

With one hand on her, he reached over and flipped a switch on the wall. A hook descended from the ceiling.

Her eyes widened. "What's going on? What are you planning?"

He hooked her wrists above her head, causing her to stand on the tips of her toes. Seeing her lithe yet supple body stretched like that, his cock throbbed. Taking a fistful of braids, he yanked her head back so he had easier access to her mouth. His lips descended on hers, hard, devouring. He poured his lust and frustration into the kiss. She couldn't keep up even if she were trying.

The heat and wetness of her mouth set him on fire. The problem with feasting on her was that he only got more ravenous.

But lest he scare her too much, he backed off, softening his kisses, gently biting and sucking on her lips, teasing her with his tongue. To get her where he wanted her to be, he needed to coax her there.

She gave a sweet moan, evidence his approach was working. He liked to think that he was part of the reason she had chosen to stay. She was obviously receptive to him on a sexual level.

But as soon as the thought passed through his head, she began to contradict him. She pulled away from his mouth.

"Don't— Have you heard back from your cousin yet?" she inquired. "How is everyone doing? How's Claire?"

"I haven't heard back," he said, trailing kisses down the side of her neck.

"Can we try them again?"

"After I'm done."

"Done with what?"

"Done with you."

Releasing her braids, he pushed her breasts up for his mouth to caress.

"Honestly, you don't have anything better to do with your time? Don't you have to...work?"

"Would you rather we go back to talking about Dawson and Carlos?"

She let out a deflated sigh. He kissed her breasts, then down the slight indent of her torso.

Unlike other chastity belts that wrapped the waist, the one she wore dipped beneath her belly button like a scoop bikini. Lowering himself, he tongued her belly button then licked the part of the belt covering her clit. She gave a whimper. He caressed her legs, feeling the backs of her thighs, her toned calves. There wasn't an inch of her that wasn't divine.

Standing back up, he cupped her face and went back to kissing her mouth. "You're so bloody sexy."

"You sweet talking me now?"

He went for her throat, sucking for a longer time than he would have on someone with lighter skin, unless he wanted to leave a hickey. Returning to her breasts, he targeted the nipples this time, playfully licking and nibbling the hardened buds. She shivered. She was surrendering to her arousal. The scent of it made him dizzy with lust. He wondered how long he could last before he fucked her silly. And he could do it without a condom now.

His hands caressed the belt. "You ready for this to come off?"

"Hell yes!"

"Then ask me to fuck you."

Her bottom lip dropped.

He grabbed her hips. "Ask me to fuck you hard."

She hesitated.

Just do it, he said to her silently as he pulled her body against his crotch.

"And if I don't?"

"You get to keep the chastity belt on."

"Is there an option C?"

"Nope."

He ground his erection against the belt.

"Why not?"

He almost laughed at the rather childish question. She knew the answer. She was just stalling.

He indulged her question. "Because I make the rules, pet."

"How does my having a chastity belt on benefit you?" she challenged.

He cupped the back of her head and drew her ear close to his mouth. "I can fuck you in the arse with the belt *on*."

She started straining against the bonds.

Remembering that she had put down a 5, the max score, for anal sex, he asked, "When was the last time you had cock up your arse?"

"A long time ago."

"What's a long time?"

"Two, two and a half years, maybe."

"I thought you liked it. Your answer to the Scarlet Auction questionnaire indicated you did."

"I think I misread that one."

More lies.

"Too bad," he said.

He released her and took a step back. If she wasn't going to give him what he wanted, she could keep the belt on longer. He would show her that she would be the one worse for wear.

He unzipped his pants and pulled out his erection. Just thinking about being buried inside her made him stiffer than anything. His cock felt so hard he could probably use it to hammer nails. Slowly, he stroked himself. He wished he had some of her natural lubrication, but his arousal was high enough he could make himself come without much effort.

Her gaze fixed upon his hand job, as if mesmerized by the rhythm of his hand going up and down his shaft. She licked her lower lip. His gaze took in the tip of her tongue, her plump, glistening lip, the swell of her hips, the smoothness of her belly.

He could go for a non-ejaculating orgasm, but he wanted to prove a point. So when the boiling in his bollocks reached its peak, he allowed his climax to shoot through him. His jism landed on her belly and splattered the belt and upper thighs. He bucked his hips, and a final spurt splashed on a breast. He shuddered as waves of hot rapture rolled through him.

When the tide had receded, he shook his head to get his bearings. He replaced his cock and zipped up his pants. For the moment, he drank in the sight of his cum marking her body, some of it starting to slide down her leg.

"Enjoy the chastity belt, pet," he said. "I'll be back later."

Resisting the urge to tear the belt off her and fondle her till she came screaming for him, he left the playroom and went to retrieve his phone. He texted Stephens:

> Get me pics of
> Sam Green.

He drew in a long breath as he thought about Kimani hanging from the ceiling. She didn't know it, but keeping the chastity belt on was the safer option. When the belt came off, things were going to get a lot harder for her.

CHAPTER ELEVEN

He had left her to stew in her juices— literally—again. Kimani could feel the wetness collected on the belt. She yanked on the shirt binding her wrists. It had no give at all. This was exactly the sort of situation she should have been avoiding.

Stupid, stupid her. She should have kept her trap shut. Now she was paying the price for her desire to be helpful. She should have walked out that door when she had the chance. Screw the scoop.

But what about Claire? She could call the cops and have them check on the cabin. But what if they didn't find anything worth investigating? She couldn't risk pissing off Jake. What if he took his anger out on Claire?

She had come this far, invested more than she had ever thought she would. She couldn't give up without seeing it through. Her life wasn't in peril, so what would her excuse be? That she was afraid of more BDSM? That was a wimpy reason to quit when there were reporters who risked their lives—had lost their lives—to bring the truth to the world.

And she wasn't fooling anyone about Ben.

She wasn't quite ready to leave him. Her body wanted him to finish what he had started. Jesus, even watching him masturbate had been hot, seeing the flush across his chiseled chest, the tightening of his muscles, the hardness of his cock.

Why hadn't she simply told him what he wanted to hear? Her pussy clenched on emptiness. She did want to be fucked, after all. By him. She wanted an encore of the sex they'd had in the shower. But she was more than a little worried. She could tell he was upset. He had mentioned punishment. Getting fucked by Ben when he was in a good mood was one thing. In a bad mood, what might he be capable of?

Good going, Kimani. How could you have let this happen?

But beating herself up wouldn't help matters. She had to focus. What were her options? Could she use willpower to stop from becoming aroused? Could she suffer through whatever torment he had in mind and eventually outlast him? He wasn't all asshole. Maybe he would have mercy on her.

Mercy. That was her safety word. He would honor it. Only a total jerk like Jake wouldn't.

Jake. She had to find out what the guy was up to and how Claire was truly doing. She probably couldn't do it without Ben. It was too dangerous to return to the cabin without him. And if she brought someone like Sam with her,

Jake probably wouldn't let them in.

She wondered if the second recording pen she'd left behind had picked up anything. And where had that first one disappeared to? It would have picked up the exchange between her and Jake on the matter of the safety word. If she was lucky, it had also picked up the incident with the shock collar, when Claire used her safety word but Jake ignored it. She had to get that pen back.

Okay, so she needed Ben to get her back to the cabin. Could she get him to do what she wanted for a change? She hated finding herself between a rock and a hard place, i.e. him, all the time. Should she be a better pet? Would that get her further? It was worth a shot. But it also meant submitting more of herself than she wanted to. Was she ready to do that?

Yes. His kisses are to die for, his caresses melt you faster than butter on burning coal, and he fucking made you squirt for the first time ever. Not to mention his cock feels so damn good inside you, you might never again be satisfied with your vibrator.

With a groan, she tried to think of something else, like the soreness of her feet from being on imaginary five-inch stilettos. When was he going to come back?

She tested the shirt again. No go. Not that he would be happy to find her out of her bonds.

Looking around the room, she remembered

that she was supposed to come up with her punishment. She wondered which of the implements would be the least harsh. The flogger hadn't been too bad. She could probably handle more of that. The cane was another story. She eyed the stocks, one tall, one short. How bad could being locked in one of those be? The shorter one would probably be more comfortable since one could kneel.

Her gaze moved next to the cages. One was tall and narrow, almost like a coffin, obviously for standing. The other was cube-shaped and cramped-looking. Even in a sitting position, she would have to bend over to prevent her head from hitting the top of it, and there was definitely not enough room to stretch one's legs. But the cages didn't look as ominous as the wooden pony. Somewhere she had read that, in medieval days, victims would be placed atop the edge with anchors tied to their ankles.

She started to get nervous. There had to be a way out of the punishment. Could she stall him? Maybe make him come until he was exhausted? But the man wasn't built like most guys she knew. Jesus, he was capable of multiple orgasms. She even had the feeling he could outlast women.

She shuddered. Maybe she could bribe him.

With what? What could you possibly offer a billionaire who has it all?

Herself. Her body. Her submission.

But a guy like him can get dozens of women willing and waiting to do his bidding. He could probably walk out the door, snap his fingers, and find women ready to jump down his pants. Hotter women. Women more experienced with BDSM.

Information.

That was the only thing she had of value, and that he clearly wanted.

One of the flat screens on the wall flickered on. A film started to play. The setting was dark, with illumination coming from a single spotlight behind a curtain. An Asian female, naked and bound in shibari, dangled from an apparatus onstage. In the audience were dozens of Japanese men in suits.

Onstage, a man held a long black dildo attached to the end of a stick. He pushed the dildo at her crotch till it slid between her folds. She winced but soon began to moan as the dildo pumped in and out of her. Across the stage, another petite woman was tied with her arms stretched above her. A man pounded his cock into her from behind.

The scene faded away into one from Nagisa Oshima's *In the Realm of the Senses*, in which the character of Kichizo Ishida receives a blow job while smoking a cigarette. The following scene was of Ishida and Sada Abe, a former prostitute, having sex while a woman played the shamisen in the background.

Kimani found herself drawn into the scenes.

They felt like porn, for they titillated, but they looked so artistic that they felt like more than porn,

The door opened. At first she was excited to see Ben, like a dog happy for its owner's return at the end of the day, but his jaw seemed a little tight, and his eyes shone with determination. Her excitement turned to trepidation.

CHAPTER TWELVE

"Already got one," had been Stephens' reply.

Prior to returning to the playroom, mobile in hand, Ben had studied the headshot Stephens had sent over of a good-looking guy in his mid to late forties. According to the background research Stephens had conducted, Samuel Green was married to Kyle Santos and had two children. That didn't mean Kimani wasn't romantically involved with the *Tribune* editor, but Ben would wager their relationship had more to do with work or education. Perhaps this Sam fellow filled a mentor role for Kimani.

"That is the man she met at the coffee shop," Wong had confirmed after Ben had forwarded the photo.

Ben had considered forwarding the photo to Ezra as well, but he didn't trust Ezra's discretion. He was fairly certain anyway that Sam was the one who had approached Ezra.

What was Kimani up to?

Ben recalled the snippets of conversation he had overheard Kimani having on his mobile with Sam. The two of them were digging into his family, probably with Uncle Gordon as the target.

Had that been her intent all along?

She couldn't know that he would show up at Jake's cabin and decide to buy her. Did she somehow know that Jason would be at the Scarlet Auction? Was that why she was an auction participant?

That seemed unlikely as well. It was a roundabout way to get access to Jason, who wasn't even that involved in his uncle's campaign. And why would she think there was anything worth investigating? Uncle Gordon was a fucking Boy Scout.

And Kimani seemed to genuinely like Gordon.

Sam had asked about the political action committee, so maybe Gordon wasn't the target. A group of developers raising more than half a million might be somewhat interesting, but it hardly seemed newsworthy. Independent expenditures, whether organized by labor or business, happened all the time. Unless Kimani and Sam were hoping to make mountains out of molehills, there was nothing to report there.

He wondered if Jason's participation in the Scarlet Auction as well as his own could hurt Uncle Gordon. The intrigue and scandal would draw attention, but, as nephews, they were a step removed from Gordon. Voters should be savvy enough to know that Gordon couldn't control what other members of his family did. Nevertheless, the political consultant might have to take a run at the scenario.

Fuck.

Buying Kimani had come with complications he hadn't expected. Whether she had set out to find dirt on the Leo family or she'd decided to take advantage of an opportunity that had fallen in her lap, Ben didn't like it.

He glanced at the monitor to see that Kimani was fixed on the screen, currently depicting a scene from *In the Realm of the Senses*, a timeless film that seemed not the slightest bit dated though it had been made in 1976. She rubbed her thighs together.

Fuck.

She looked so hot. He couldn't wait to sink himself, sans a condom, into her.

He headed for the playroom and threw open the door. When her gaze met his, he could see the hunger of lust in her eyes, and that turned him on as much of anything.

"Please fuck me."

Surprised, he raised his brows.

"Fuck me hard."

It was music to his ears. The hottest thing he had ever heard. His emotions ran high at her statement, half plea, half demand. He wanted nothing more than to give her what she wanted. He wanted to see her come, wanted to see her brow furrowed in passion, wanted to hear her scream out his name.

But first, he had something to take care of.

Stepping to her, he grabbed her by the jaw and lifted her chin. "You say it so well. Say it again."

Her eyes were dark pools of shiny arousal.

"Fuck me hard. Master."

His cock throbbed.

"Again."

"Fuck me hard, Master."

"More. Beg like you mean it."

"Please, Master, please fuck me. Your pet needs to be fucked so badly. Please let me have your cock inside me. Please, Master!"

This was an unexpected turn of events, but good.

Releasing her jaw, he retrieved the key from his pocket and unlocked the chastity belt. The scent of her hit him hard, making the blood flow through him fast and hot. He let the belt drop to the floor and felt for her wetness.

"You're nice and ready for cock, aren't you?"

She closed her eyes as his fingers grazed her clitoris. "Yes, Master, I am."

He dipped a finger into her channel. Feeling her sodden heat, he had to take a calming breath. She moaned as he withdrew his digit. She swayed her hips, and for a while he allowed her to hump his hand. He plunged two fingers into her pussy, and easily found her swollen G-spot. Her groans grew louder. He pulled his fingers out and shoved them into her mouth. She licked and sucked.

"Good pet," he praised.

After she had cleaned off his fingers, he bent down and picked up the belt and placed it atop a dresser. Opening one of the drawers, he pulled out a vibrating egg and its accompanying controller. He slipped the remote control into his pocket, remembering that he still had the remote and shock collar that Jake had used on Claire. He didn't rule out using the collar on Kimani, but he would wait on it for now. He had other toys at his disposal.

Before he inserted the egg, he kissed her first. Kissing got her juices flowing, he had noticed. And he loved that something so simple, something that was just him, without accessories, could have such an effect on her. It got *him* going as well.

He grabbed a fistful of braids and pulled her head back as he tongued or bit every inch of her mouth. With his other hand, he rubbed the egg between her clit and folds. When he placed it at her slit, her cunt eagerly sucked up the egg. Her kisses grew more urgent. Reaching into his pocket for the remote, he turned the egg on to its lowest setting while he continued to devour her mouth.

He increased the vibration. Distracted by the sensations that were filling her cunt, she stopped kissing and moaned against his lips.

"Jesus, that feels *good*," she whispered.

"Does it, pet?" he murmured on her lips. "I can make it feel even better."

"Yeah?"

He dialed the vibration up a couple notches and watched her lashes flutter, her lips part, her breath become erratic.

Her eyes grew wide. "Oh...wow..."

"All you got to do is tell me what you know about De Reyes and Chang."

"Wh...?"

"You're not someone who talks for the sake of talking. There's something you're not telling me."

He could tell she had trouble thinking, so he decreased the vibration. "Dawson Chang and Carlos De Reyes. What do you know?"

"They're colleagues."

He yanked her hair hard. "Don't fuck with me by telling me shit I already know."

Her eyes flashed in anger. "Why do you keep thinking I know something?"

"Are you suggesting you've been completely truthful with me?"

She didn't say anything.

"Thought so," he muttered, releasing her and returning the vibration to its lowest setting.

He walked over to the wall and flipped a switch. The hook began to rise, pulling her a few feet off the floor before stopping.

"What are you doing?" she asked with apprehension.

"I'm going to get the truth one way or another. It's up to you how long you want the torment to last."

CHAPTER THIRTEEN

What the...?

This was not good. Dangling in the air had transferred the pressure from her toes to her arms but not necessarily for the better. Kimani wriggled, trying to find a way back down to the ground. How the hell was she going to get herself out of this predicament?

Wait. Had he mentioned "torment" again?

A jolt of vibration through her lower body caused her to shudder. Her thoughts scattered. She tried to rein them back in. She couldn't escape without them.

But the vibrations felt *so good.* She was sure she could come any minute now. All that time left to herself with erotic imagery on the screen had built tension that desperately wanted release.

Hadn't she been a good pet? Didn't she ask to be fucked, beg for his cock like he'd wanted her to?

She moaned as the vibrations faded once more to a faint and dull hum, enough to keep her arousal front and center but not enough to send her over the edge.

Ben unbuttoned and removed his shirt. She

swept her gaze appreciatively over his chiseled chest and scrumptious six-pack, wishing she could run her hands over every muscle.

Stop drooling, Kimani, and focus on getting yourself outta here.

Right. What could she do? Convincing him that he was wrong, that he only imagined she knew something, wasn't working out.

She watched him select a flogger from the wall. Shit.

The flogger had about two dozen leather falls. He whipped the flogger against her leg.

"Ooof!"

Okay, maybe this one could be bad. This flogger stung more, though she wasn't sure why. The vibrations from the egg flared before settling back down.

So this was the torment he had in mind. Flogging and orgasm denial.

"Is my safety word still the same?" she inquired.

"Good you asked. It's not. Your safety word is telling me what I want to know about De Reyes and Chang."

"What?! That's got to be against the rules."

"You have an out. That's all I need to provide."

"But your 'out' is extortion!"

"Guess that makes me an asshole," he replied, landing the flogger against her thighs.

She yelped, then gave a frustrated cry. She

tried to free herself but could only kick at air.

Why did you trust the guy? Why didn't you run the hell away when you had the chance?

She narrowed her eyes. "Not only is it extortion, it's not fair."

"Life's not fair, pet."

"And it's *playing low*. Is this how you conduct your business, too? Ugh. Ow!"

He had struck her twice on the ass. Hard.

The vibrations surged again.

"Arm-twisting and coercion," she continued. "Getting what you want without caring what happens to others. You know, stuff like that gives rich people a bad name."

He paused. "For the record, I rarely employ coercion and arm-twisting as business strategies. There are plenty of businessmen who have succeeded through bullying, but my father built his success on creating win-win situations for all parties."

He ran a hand gently over the arch of her ass, as if admiring it. "See, if you tell me what you know, you get to have some bloody fine orgasms. Win-win."

"But how is *torment* a win for me?" she seethed, trying to ignore the fact that his thumb now rubbed her clit, causing a delicious agitation to ripple through her.

Retracting his thumb, he sucked it, tasting her. "I can see how you got into Stanford."

Her anger, fueled by helplessness and fear,

flared at his patronization. "Fuck you."

His brows went up, and she immediately regretted her words. She rarely used those two words together. In fact, she couldn't remember the last time she had told anyone to fuck off. Not even the time she and her friend Jasmine had been falsely accused of shoplifting by a store employee who'd said that the missing necklace "had to have been taken by *those* women." Turned out another employee had put the necklace on a mannequin.

"Let's see what your education is worth," Ben said. "Is it very smart of you to defy me?"

She sighed. "I don't know anything!"

"Problem is, I don't believe you. And the longer you hold out, the more significant your information must be. I'd say whatever it is you know must be pretty juicy. Were De Reyes and Chang lovers?"

"How the hell would I know?"

"You tell me."

She let out a frustrated growl, then cried out when he snapped the flogger against her rear.

"Is this what you want on your conscience?" she tried. "The torture of an innocent victim?"

"You're not innocent, pet."

The flogger fell several more times, followed by an increase in vibration. She shivered at the beautiful ripples resounding off her pussy walls.

"And 'victim' is a loaded word. You're only a victim if you suffer something you don't want."

She couldn't believe this guy. "You're saying I *want* this?"

"You haven't used your out yet, so I assume you prefer the flogging."

At that, he flogged her breasts, making her gasp at how near the leather straps landed to her nipples. That was one place she did *not* want to get hit.

"Preferring something doesn't mean I *want* it. I would *prefer* to have a root canal over getting my fingers cut off, but who the hell wants a root canal?"

"You can argue your case all you want; I bet you'd make a great lawyer. It doesn't change your options."

The vibrations grew to their highest level yet, melting the tension inside her and boiling it all at the same time.

Think! You're supposed to be thinking of a way out!

Maybe she could make up something about Carlos and Dawson. Their being lovers or ex-lovers was a good explanation. But she couldn't bring herself to spread a rumor like that. And what if Ben found out it wasn't true? She did not want to face the repercussions of that. Was there something more innocuous that she could tell him?

The sting of the flogger erased all thought from her mind. Once again, it was followed by a surge of vibration, liquefying her insides and making her a molten mess from which a climax began to rise.

The vibrations stopped.

No!

She cried out as Ben resumed whipping her. She tried to angle her body away from the blows, but sometimes she only made it worse. When he stopped flogging, her body was on edge for the reward of vibration to follow.

It didn't this time. Her arousal screamed with the frustration of a child used to getting what she wanted but being told "no" for the first time. Where were the vibrations? She might come this time.

Jesus, help me.

"You don't have to be an asshole," she murmured. "You're not like Jake. If what you said about the way you do business is true, then you know how to play fair. You're a good guy."

"Nice try, pet. You don't get to accuse me of *playing low* then try to flatter me. That good-cop-bad-cop strategy doesn't work when there's only one of you."

The flogger struck her legs, her ass, her tits. This time the flogger grazed her nipple. She screamed out. The vibrations returned, in unison with the blows. Now she didn't know whether to dread or welcome the flogger. After several more hits, he paused but allowed the vibrations to continue. Her body was warm all over, her pussy grasping onto the egg as if her life depended upon it, anxious for the orgasm that would wash away the tension before the flogger fell once more.

So close...so close...

Her head fell back in defeat when the vibrations ceased. She hung her head, tired from the roller coaster of pleasure and pain.

"Ready to use your out?" he inquired.

"I don't have anything to tell you," she moaned.

"I don't believe you."

She looked at him, bewildered. "Then I'm screwed. I'm fucked."

He stared intently into her eyes. "Yeah, babe, you are."

CHAPTER FOURTEEN

Maybe he was wrong. Maybe she didn't have any secret about De Reyes and Chang to reveal.

No. Ben trusted his instincts. She had hesitated once too often for him to believe she was completely innocent.

Knowing her arms would be sore, he said, "Let's try something different for fun."

Flipping one of the switches on the wall, he brought her back down to the floor.

"How can I prove to you I don't have anything on Carlos and Dawson?" she asked as he unhooked her wrists and undid the shirt binding them.

"You can't if it's not the truth," he said gravely before dragging her over to the wooden table.

"Our week together is just supposed to be about sex. I didn't sign up for anything else—especially extortion!"

He tossed her onto the table and held her down by the throat. "You sure you want to go down that path, pet?"

He wanted to point out that *she* had started it all with her phone calls to Sam, but he didn't want to scare her too much. She might shut down and call an end to their week. What would he do if she did?

He didn't want to let her go. For a variety of reasons. But he couldn't falsely imprison her. That would be a felony in California and could impact the family far worse than any scandal over a sex auction.

She tried to pull him off her. A fruitless endeavor. And even slightly entertaining. As fit and strong as she was, she had no chance against his strength, fueled by both ardor and anger.

A pair of scarlet leather cuffs dangled from one edge of the table. He grabbed them and fit one over her wrist. He had to let go of her throat to secure the cuff. She tried to scramble away, kicking him in the stomach, but he shoved her back down onto the table. He surprised her with his roughness, and he took her moment of pause to cuff her other wrist. But she wasn't done struggling and almost kneed him in the groin.

He pinched a nipple and twisted it hard. Her brow furrowed in pain, and her mouth fell open.

"Behave yourself," he warned. Seeing that defiance still shone in her eyes, he added, "You want to do this the hard way? I'm happy to play hard, pet."

She frowned but made no further movement. He pushed himself off the table. All her writhing beneath him had caused his blood to boil. God, he wanted to fuck her so badly.

After getting two cords of rope, he bound each of her legs to a leg of the table before stepping back to survey the length of her beautiful body stretched over the surface. Apparently she had come to her senses, for she hadn't fought him this time. As a reward, he turned the vibrating egg back on. He retrieved a set of sheer black nipple cups, a bag of clothespins and string.

"Where are those going?" she asked.

He caressed her side, from her breast to her hip. "If you don't want to give up the information I want right away, I'm okay with that. There's nothing on my schedule but you, pet."

"Why are you so damn convinced I know anything?"

He debated telling her what he knew, what he had seen and heard, but he didn't want to show his hand just yet. There was time.

His hand went lower, past her hip to her thigh. She had such baby-soft skin. Perfectly smooth. Perfectly unblemished. Despite the flogging it had received. She was a canvas waiting to be painted upon.

"You tell me," he said.

She rolled her eyes at his non-answer, then gasped when he cupped her mound, grazing his digits over her folds.

"Oh, oh!" she huffed, grimacing when he

dragged a finger along her clit.

"Better turn this off," he said of the egg. "Don't want you coming."

She groaned when the vibrations stopped. He watched the heaving of her chest before taking up the nipple cups. He lubricated the rims of the cups to create better suction. Squeezing one, he placed it over a nipple and gently released it.

The cup pulled her nipple and part of the areola inside. Her brow furrowed. He tugged on the cup to test it would stay, then applied the second one to her other nipple. He had chosen larger cups, which created more suction.

Next came the zipper of clothespins. He pinched the side of her breast and affixed a clothespin over the string.

"Ow," she murmured, her breathing shallow.

By the time he was done, he had attached half a dozen clothespins from her breast to her rib. He did the same to her other side. Stepping back, he admired his handiwork.

She looked gorgeous.

Not able to hold out, he undid his pants and let them fall to the ground. He grabbed his cock and pulled hard. He rubbed the pre-cum over the crown, imagining her hot wetness coating his shaft. There would be no condom in the way this time.

He jerked himself to coming without ejaculating, then closed his eyes to let the euphoria settle back down. He opened his eyes to find her studying him. Stepping out of his pants, he took out the rcmote to the egg and grabbed a wand massager before standing at the end of the table. Turning it on, he ran it down the middle of her torso and over her belly. Her lashes fluttered.

"What kind of vibrator do you keep?" he asked.

"A Hitachi."

"What setting do you use?"

He pulled the nipple cup fairly hard, but it remained securely attached to her tit.

"Medium, I guess. I start off low, though."

He put the wand to her pussy. "Like that?"

She purred.

"That a good setting?"

She nodded.

"Ever go to the max?"

She shook her head.

"Ever have more than one vibrator going at once?"

Another shake of the head.

Taking up the remote, he turned on the egg. Her mouth fell open as her pussy received vibrations inside and out. It wasn't going to take her long to come. Her back arched off the table. Soft wails and pants escaped her lips.

Before she went over the peak, however, he turned everything off, leaving her bereft and quaking with confusion. She shut her eyes in concentration, as if willing her body over the edge into orgasm. He slapped her to fix her attention back on him.

"De Reyes and Chang," he said.

It took her a few seconds to comprehend what was going on.

"I don't..." was all she said.

He turned the wand back on, but instead of returning it to her pussy, he broke the suction and removed one of the nipple cups and put the wand to her engorged nipple.

She shrieked when the wand came into contact with the overly sensitive bud. The chain to her cuffs rattled as she strained away from the vibrations. Holding her down, he pressed the wand to her nipple, which, he remembered, was sensitive to begin with. The suction of the nipple cup had magnified the sensitivity at least twofold, judging from her reaction.

"Ahhh!" she cried out.

"You know your out," he replied.

Her body bucked, trying to shake off his hand.

"Mercy!"

"That's not it."

She glared at him, rightfully angry. He had never ignored a safety word before.

He removed the other nipple cup, turned the setting on the wand higher and ground it into her nipple.

She would have leaped out of her skin if she

could.

"Fuck! Ahhh!" she sobbed.

He decided to give her some relief. He could be a sadistic son of a bitch, but he wasn't a pure sadist. Turning the setting back down, he put the wand to her clit. Her harsh gasps soon turned to liquid moans. He kept the wand at her clit till pleasure washed away discomfort. The adrenalin would be coursing heavily through her, amplifying her arousal. His groin tightened. There was nothing sexier than a woman ready to come, wanting to come.

"Ohhhh," she cooed as the wand worked its magic.

"It's going to feel so good when you come," he encouraged.

She moaned in agreement.

"That orgasm is waiting for you. It's yours. All you have to do is give me the truth."

She moaned in despair.

He took away the wand and turned it off. "You're so close to coming, pet. I can see it in the way your body quivers."

She took several shaky breaths before saying, "What happened to fucking me?"

Her response surprised him.

"Didn't I ask—didn't I beg for it?" she added.

He stared into her eyes. She meant it. And it was so fucking hot.

He didn't mind the shy women, whose demure glances hinted that they wanted to be taken. But he liked his women bold. Unafraid to verbalize what they wanted. It was different from the culture he had grown up with

And of course he wanted to fuck her. He could do nothing else but fuck her for the rest of the day. But he wasn't done toying with her. What was a Dom to do?

CHAPTER FIFTEEN

By his pause, Kimani guessed that he hadn't expected her response. Most likely he expected her to give in. She *wanted* to give in. She wanted to come so badly—so, *so* badly. Her body had been dangling on the edge for so long. It deserved to let go and fall into the pool of carnal bliss.

"Fuck me," she dared.

He blinked several times. He seemed to hesitate. She had never seen him unsure of himself.

"You sure you want that, pet?" he returned.

It was her turn to doubt. But she didn't want to return to the nipple torture. And maybe, if he was buried inside her, he would want to stay until he orgasmed, and hopefully she would, too.

"Fuck me already," she spat, before he changed his mind.

Setting aside the wand, he yanked her as close to the edge of the table as the cuffs would allow. He took out the egg and rammed his cock in its place.

The force of it made her teeth chatter. Maybe she had spoken too soon.

The following thrusts were gentler, and she exalted in the sensation of being filled by him and nothing but him, flesh to flesh. He felt so good. So, so good. The only thing she could do without were the clothespins. They jiggled whenever he thrust into her, accentuating the pinch. But the rapture he coaxed held sway over any discomfort.

Until he tugged on the string.

He wasn't going to pull the clothespins off, was he? Then again, the string was there for a reason.

"De Reyes and Chang," he reminded her. "Or, Carlos and Dawson, as you seem to prefer."

Shit. She had hoped he'd forgotten. What could she say? She had run out of ideas. Or her current state didn't make it easy to access any ideas that could be had.

"If I had anything worth telling..." she began.

...*I would.* But it was getting harder to lie to him. He seemed to know when she was lying. Maybe she wasn't a good liar.

She tried a different strategy. "I could be a good pet. A very good pet, Master."

"Yeah?" he responded with interest.

"I could suck your cock whenever you wanted."

He shoved harder into her.

Encouraged, she said, "Your cock is so tasty, I could suck it all day long, Master."

"Anytime? Anywhere?"

"Yes, Master."

"What else?"

"What else would Master want?"

"Your arse."

She hesitated. It had been a while since she'd had anal sex. And her last boyfriend had had a long but more narrow cock.

"If that's what Master wants."

Leaning over her, he wound some of her braids into his fist. "Say it like you mean it."

"You can have my ass."

"Beg for it."

"Please take my ass."

"You can do better."

"Please fuck my ass, Master."

"Convince me."

His other hand had slipped between their bodies. He fondled her clit with his thumb.

"I haven't been anal fucked in years," she murmured, loving the stimulation on her clit while his cock stroked her inside. "My ass is nice and tight. Ready to be stretched by you, Master."

He plunged himself deeper into her.

"And you want my ass," she continued. "I bet you wanted it the instant you saw it."

With a groan, he slammed his hips at her several times, rattling her to the core. Letting go of her hair, he grabbed her ass, dragging her back to the edge of the table so he could drill himself farther into her. She could hear the wetness of her pussy in the juicy slaps of flesh against flesh.

He grunted, and his body jerked in small spasms. She surmised he was coming.

To her relief, he backed down. The pounding had been a little too hard for her to focus on her pleasure. His thrusting having eased, she could now feel her own climax building. He dragged his cock in and out of her, making her shiver with every stroke.

Please, please let me come this time.

"My pet wants to come, doesn't she?"

Before she could stop herself, she whimpered. He smiled and caressed her clit with his thumb.

O.M.G.

"Please," she whispered, "can I come?"

"You know the answer to that."

God help me.

She stared into his eyes, pleading even though she didn't want to.

A bloodcurdling cry tore from her mouth when he pulled the string, sending the clothespins flying.

"Motherfucker!" she grunted, then braced herself for the second unzipping.

But instead of the string, he reached for the wand and turned it on. She almost sobbed when pleasure started flowing from her nether regions. Her poor confused body didn't know what to make of it all. There was pain. Then pleasure.

Then pain. Then pleasure. Sometimes, the pain and pleasure even started to meld together.

"Ready to use your out?" he asked.

I can't.

Taking the string, he ripped off the other clothespins. This time she was prepared for how much it would smart, but she still wailed at the snapping of the clothespins.

I'm done. I can't take any more.

Her body was on fire in so many different ways, she didn't know what she wanted. The world before her blurred.

"You want to tell me what you know or should we go on to round two?"

She turned to look at him. For what felt like several minutes, they stared at one another in silence. His eyes beseeched her: *tell me.*

Slowly, she shook her head in answer.

"Fuck," he swore to himself.

Turning on the wand, he put it to her clit. His cock was still hard, still buried inside her. Holding the wand in place, he rocked his hips.

The vibrations had never felt so good. *He* had never felt so good. The combination was the most marvelous thing she had ever felt. She needed this and didn't care how high she would go, born on waves of the finest rapture. Somewhere, a warning voice cautioned that this was just the beginning of the next torment, that he wasn't going to let her come. But she had already surrendered to the scintillation building between her legs.

"Come, Kimani," he ordered.

She would have come with or without his permission, thrust to the heights of bliss. She cried out this time in ecstasy. When he pulled out, she felt wetness stream from her and heard it splash upon the floor. Her body shuddered in pleasure and relief.

He speared himself back into her, thrusting, pushing her back up that orgasmic plateau. A new stream of wetness gushed from her when he jerked out before slamming himself back in. She heard his roar, felt him trembling, and then a new and separate heat filled her. He bucked against her several times, driving himself deeper, the throbbing of his cock stretching her.

He had come, but she wasn't sure if that was a good thing or not.

CHAPTER SIXTEEN

*F*uck. Why the hell wouldn't she just tell him what he wanted to know?

He stayed inside her, relishing the contractions of her pussy about his cock. She felt fucking amazing. There was nothing like being in her hot, wet pussy.

But he wasn't supposed to have let her come. Especially since she hadn't asked to come. He could tell she wanted it, though, and he wanted to give it to her. Maybe because he felt guilty about being such a prick. But since when did being a prick bother him?

Frustrated, he decided not to dwell on it. Instead, he turned up the vibration on the wand, which was still at her clit. Her eyes widened, unsure if she wanted the stimulation on the tender bud. She squirmed atop the table, half wanting to avoid the wand, but it didn't take long for her arousal to reignite. She tensed and strained as another orgasm coiled within her. It unwound, making her scream and sending her body into spasms.

He loved watching her come undone. His cock, still buried in her sweet pussy, stirred.

"Okay, okay, enough," she pleaded through chattering teeth.

He turned off the wand and withdrew from her. Undoing the ropes and cuffs, he pulled her up into a sitting position and wrapped his arms about her.

"You let me come," she murmured, tired from the exertions.

"Doesn't mean we're done," he replied, unsure of what to make of himself. When he said he was going to do something, he saw it through. Why, then, hadn't he done it with her?

"Look," she said, "I'll tell you this: Carlos and Dawson have a history. What I know was told to me in confidence, and I can't betray that. I just can't."

He let out a long breath. Looking into her eyes, he saw that whatever she knew, she wasn't going to give it up. A part of him wanted to test how much she could take, but he was just going to cement his status as an asshole if he tormented her further. Being an asshole wouldn't bother him, but he worried that she would hate him for it.

"All right, I'll take that," he relented. "For now."

"Would you mind if I used your cellphone?"

He bristled at the thought of her calling Sam.

"I want to see if I can talk to Claire," she clarified.

He helped her off the table and gave her back her t-shirt.

"Do I get to put on real underwear?" she asked after slipping on the shirt.

"I like you without."

"If we had used a condom, I might be okay with that. But I don't want to be, uh, leaking stuff wherever I walk."

"Right." He smiled at the thought that he had ejaculated inside her, leaving his mark.

In the living room, he dug through the purchases Beth had made and tossed Kimani a lacy black thong.

"There anything else?" she asked.

"You want the chastity belt back on?"

"Fine."

She gawked at the price tag before removing it and sliding the thong on. He grabbed his mobile and dialed Jason.

"You can take the call here," he told Kimani.

No more secretive calls for you, pet.

"Hey, cuz, you coming back or what?" Jason inquired. "Jake's pissed that you haven't brought his second slut back yet."

"She's not his. Where's Claire?"

"Who? Oh, you mean Jake's slut. She's doing some naked sunbathing with the other sluts."

"Give her your phone. Montana wants to talk to her."

"Jake's sleeping. He's been totally wasted."

"So?"

"Shouldn't I get his permission to let his slut

talk on the phone?"

"Just give her your mobile."

"Okay, cuz."

Ben handed his mobile to Kimani before making his way to the bathroom to run a bath for her. There were a plethora of bath paraphernalia the maid had stocked, none of which he ever used, but he selected a scented bath bomb to toss into the water. He returned to the kitchen to pour two glasses of water.

"Are you sure you're doing okay?" Kimani asked.

Ben picked up his iPad. Stephens had sent him a copy of the contract Jake had signed with the Scarlet Auction. At Ben's direction, Stephens had also had Ben's personal attorney review the documents. Jake was right. There was a clause prohibiting the involvement of third parties not authorized by the Scarlet Auction, with a hefty financial penalty for violating any terms of the contract. Ben's attorney didn't think there was a way around the contract, and suggested that Jake try to negotiate an amendment or that Ben himself seek authorization from the Scarlet Auction.

Kimani frowned. "Did Lisa and Ryan get burned, too?"

Ben didn't think Jake would go through the trouble of renegotiating his contract, and Ben didn't have the patience or inclination to jump through whatever hoops the Scarlet Auction would require. He thought about paying Jake more, but he had already shelled out a ridiculous amount of money to have Kimani for a week.

Looking over at her, he eyed the tight fit of her shirt and her shapely legs. He recalled how gloriously she squirted.

If he had to, he'd buy her all over again.

"What else did he do?" she asked.

But she wasn't just a fucktoy. She was working an angle. Even though she wasn't on the payroll of the *Tribune*, she and this Sam Green were up to something.

Ben set aside the iPad. He might have let the proverbial fox into the henhouse. Allowed a budding journalist to join him and Uncle Gordon for lunch. But it had been positive. Kimani seemed to genuinely like Uncle Gordon, and she had given him a lead on De Reyes and Chang. He preferred to evaluate for himself the relationship she alluded to, but he trusted her judgment. She could have made it easy on herself, but she hadn't.

The fact that the Lee family corporation was seeking to redevelop property in Oakland was public knowledge. His meeting with Dawson Chang would surprise no one, and he hadn't told Uncle Gordon anything at lunch that Dawson didn't already know. What could Kimani report, other than the fact he and Jason had purchased sex through the Scarlet Auction?

"Call me whenever you want—and it could be about anything, okay?" Kimani said.

"I've got a bath ready for you," he told her when she had hung up. He handed her the glass of water, which she drank without prompting. "How's Claire?"

"Okay, except that she got burned from the wax play. Jake is bad news. I doubt she signed up to get burned."

"It might not have been intentional. He may have been using shitty candles or didn't know he was holding them too close to her body. A lot of BDSM beginners don't realize the dangers of playing incorrectly. They see some scene in a movie and think there's nothing to it."

She crossed her arms. "You Jake's brah now?"

"Hell no."

"Then why are you making excuses for him?"

"I'm not making excuses. I'm just presenting another possible explanation for what happened."

"I don't trust him."

"He can be a wanker," he conceded.

"Would you entrust your sister to him?"

"Not in a million years."

She gave him a there-you-have-it look.

"But I wouldn't entrust my sisters to a guy like me, either," he said, taking her by the arm and leading her to the bathroom.

"That's comforting."

He chuckled. "Well, maybe May could take me on. You're doing all right."

He wouldn't have paid two hundred thousand for her if he didn't think she could hold up.

"I've never taken a bath with a view before," she commented when he flipped the switch to open the curtains that covered the windows surrounding one side of the tub. She took in the panoramic view of the Golden Gate Bridge, San Francisco Bay, the Palace of Fine Arts, Alcatraz, and the Presidio. "It's amazing."

He helped her out of her shirt and thong. Seeing and scenting her sex, he felt his arousal rear its head. He turned off the water and watched her nestle into the tub.

"The button next to you turns on the jets," he told her.

She pushed the button. The water gurgled and rolled.

He had thought to make a call to his lobbyist to look further into De Reyes and Chang, though when he saw Kimani sink farther into the water and her eyes roll to the back of her head as she inhaled the steam, he wanted to climb into the tub with her instead.

But she could probably benefit from some time alone. He tried not to imagine how good her slick, wet body would feel against his. How he would make her sit on his cock. He had once bent a woman over the side of the tub and banged her from behind while dunking her head into the bath water.

"After you're done," he said, "get dressed. We have dinner reservations."

"Not Ishikawa West?" she asked, looking very relaxed in the hot water.

"You have a problem with kaiseki cuisine?"

"No, I just didn't think it was possible to call up one of San Francisco's most exclusive restaurants and expect to get same-day reservations."

"You can when you're one of the top investors."

"Oh. Lucky you."

Her response nettled him. He was accustomed to women gushing at what his wealth could afford. She knew Ishikawa West was a hot restaurant, but maybe she didn't know that the establishment had earned three Michelin stars and that the waitlist was over a month long. Maybe then she'd give him some props.

No, she wouldn't. Just like she had been awed by the view from his penthouse, but it didn't transfer to him. What did it take to impress this woman? Courtside seats to a Warriors game? He could get those.

He stopped himself. He had never had proactively impress a woman before. Why was he doing it now?

Fuck.

*****

"You bringing my slut back or what?" Jake asked.

"What's the hurry?" Ben replied into his mobile.

"I told you it's against the rules."

"So?"

"So..."

Ben could hear the agitation in Jake's breathing.

"So I want her back," Jake finished.

"I paid for a full week. I want the full week."

"Fine, I'll give you back part of your money."

"Not interested in the money."

"Why you want this slut so badly? You're in the city right now. I bet you could pick up a hotter fucktoy than her. Hell, you could probably get a dozen, right? And if you're looking for black pussy, just go down to Hunters Point."

"Why are *you* so keen to have her back?"

"It's boring with just one slut. And like I said, it's against the Scarlet Auction rules."

"Why did you sell her to me in the first place?"

"I didn't read the contract that carefully. Derek, uh, mentioned it."

Bullshit. Ben was willing to bet that Derek hadn't read the contract carefully either.

"We can talk about it when I return," Ben said, seeing another call come in.

"When is that?"

"I haven't decided."

"Today would be good."

"Today won't work. I'm busy."

He still had to see to Kimani's punishment, and he wanted all his equipment at his disposal for that.

"Busy with what?" Jake huffed.

"I've got another call coming in. Let's talk tomorrow."

"But—"

Ben ended the call and picked up the incoming one.

"We can have poll results for you in two days," the pollster told Ben. "My guess is that Gordon will take a brief hit but a small one. Voters know he doesn't have control over what other members of his family do. If you were his son, maybe I'd be more worried, but even then, if the city can elect a guy who got caught with a prostitute to the school board, they can swallow a mayoral candidate with a few randy nephews."

"What about the development?"

"By the time your project gets to public comment, the news will be too old to make an impact."

"What if the issue isn't sex, but a committee of developers supporting Uncle Gordon?"

"You'll have to give me more details. Gordon is already painted as the pro-business candidate. That would cement him in that role, even if he isn't."

"I'll get back to you on details."

Kimani entered just as he hung up with the pollster. She was wrapped in a towel and was looking over the clothing options.

"Ishikawa West, hunh?" she asked.

"You might want to wear something other than the Warriors shirt."

"Don't worry. I'm not going to embarrass you."

He surveyed her. "Actually, you can go in the towel for all I care."

She sucked in her breath, probably wondering if he would make her do just that. He let her think it.

"I'm going to shower and change," he said, stowing the itch to whip the towel off her.

He was glad for the solitude of the shower. The more time he spent with her, the more he wanted her. Hell, maybe giving her back to Jake would be a good thing.

He'd had enough orgasms that his balls weren't blue anymore. And as much as he enjoyed fucking Kimani, it was getting too complicated. There was all her furtive shit, and he just wasn't himself with her. He was playing fast and loose with a reporter of some kind. And it wasn't smart.

CHAPTER SEVENTEEN

en's assistant had thought of everything, Kimani concluded as she went through all the shopping bags to find clothes, lingerie, shoes, cosmetics and toiletries. She shook her head. All this for a week of sex.

She wanted her own clothes. To feel like herself and not some guy's toy doll that he got to dress up and fuck whenever he wanted, however he wanted.

She shivered, recalling the intense orgasm she'd had while tied down on the table. She could have done without the zipper of clothespins and the nipple torture with the wand. Unwrapping the towel, she saw that her nipples had yet to fully settle back down. She couldn't believe how big and hard they had gotten with those suction cups.

The bath had relaxed and rejuvenated her, but it had been a long day. A day full of arousal and agitation, torment and ecstasy. And the day wasn't over. They hadn't even gotten to her punishment.

Shit. This was a bigger mess than she had ever thought possible.

He knew. Somehow, he knew there was

more to the story behind Dawson and Carlos. She couldn't persuade him to believe otherwise. She didn't understand why he was so convinced she was keeping the truth from him.

And the bastard had tried to torture the truth out of her. He was back to being an asshole in her book. A big fucking asshole.

The anger that had been missing the past few hours finally rose. She had been so focused on surviving all that he was doing to her body, craving and hoping to escape through the orgasm that had lain just beyond her reach.

And he had given it to her. Coming had never felt so glorious, so deserved. The tension had built up so much within her that she'd worried her body would be blown to smithereens by the climax.

So maybe the torment had been worth it. All that apprehension, all that pain had gotten the adrenaline going within her, and maybe that was what had the high so high.

He had allowed her to go there without giving up the information he sought. Is that why she wasn't as angry with him as she ought to be? Was she suffering from some twisted case of Stockholm Syndrome?

She would never have done what he did. But what had he done? To try to get what he wanted, he had used BDSM and sex—which she supposedly consented to when she'd signed up for the Scarlet Auction.

Once again, a small voice told her that she should get the hell out. Give up on the scoop. Get away from *him*. She couldn't trust what he might do next, could she?

She looked over at the door. It would be so easy. All she had to do was walk out. He wouldn't try to track her down. She felt pretty sure of it.

And somehow that belief saddened her.

Which was crazy stupid. She remembered how it had felt to give in to his seduction back at the cabin. Like falling off a cliff. And he had just shown that doing so was much more dangerous than she had ever imagined. It shouldn't matter that he could give her the most incredible orgasms. They were just orgasms.

Her anger made her want to rebel. Screw his clothes, his fancy restaurant, and anything else he wanted.

But some other part of her—sappier, stupider, more primitive—didn't want to leave him just yet. She could make herself feel better by telling herself it was her concern for Claire, the scoop, her career, determination, and persistence that made her stick around instead of bolting through the door to freedom. But that didn't explain it all.

Turning back to the offerings of haute couture, she picked out a white cocktail dress with a halter top. The dress molded her curves, but not in skin-tight fashion, and came down to mid-thigh. She opted for seamless red satin boyshort underpants. Her first choice in shoes didn't quite fit her, so she had to opt for the strappy gold sandals with five-inch heels. She debated whether to put on any makeup. Part of her didn't want to look her best for him. Part of her did.

Splitting the baby, she decided to go into the powder room to put on a little lip gloss and a touch of mascara. Nothing else. This wasn't a date.

Just dinner at the newest, most exclusive restaurant in the city.

But for someone like Ben, it probably wasn't anything special. No different than going out to a nice restaurant she and her friends might choose for a special birthday but that was well within everyone's price range.

Why was he taking her out to dinner anyway?

Because he doesn't feel like cooking. Or making her cook. Maybe she hadn't impressed him with her cooking skills at the cabin. No need to read anything into the fact that they were going out to dinner.

Back in the living room, she found a matching clutch even though she didn't have anything to put in it. Even if she had her wallet, she'd let him pick up the bill for dinner. She wasn't going to expense it and have Sam pay for what would be a very pricey meal.

Feeling nervous, she took in several deep breaths. She couldn't remember feeling this agitated about a date, and this wasn't even a date. She didn't have to impress or seduce anyone. At the end of the week, they were parting ways. No ifs, ands or buts.

Hearing his footsteps, she turned around.

She had to pick her mouth up off the ground. With his hair still slightly wet and his simple white shirt partially unbuttoned, he looked so *hot.*

And you were thinking of walking out that door, you crazy woman.

He stopped as if struck. And her ego took a leap to see that she'd had the same effect on him. She half expected to see that hungry, wolfish look. Instead, he looked awed.

"Nice dress," he said with a slight hitch in his voice.

She felt herself blushing.

But don't forget this is the guy who ripped clothespins off your body.

Trying not to care what he thought of her, she replied, "Nice, um, shoes."

"Thanks."

Setting aside his blazer, he reached for a garment bag and pulled out a woman's trench coat. "You'll need it. It's San Francisco."

She nodded and let him put the leopard-print coat on her. He swept her braids out of the collar, his knuckles grazing the back of her

150

neck. She felt his gaze but couldn't meet it, worried that she would lose all her resolve if she did. But he grasped her chin, making her look at him.

He scanned her, his pupils dilated so that his eyes were almost completely black. "I'm tempted to cancel the reservations."

Her breath was too uneven for words. As she stared into the brightness of his eyes, she reminded herself that she should hate this guy. *He's an asshole, remember? Don't let him get away with it just because he's hot and can afford nice clothes and fancy dinners.*

But don't resent him for it either. It's not his fault he's gorgeous. And you like his wicked ways. You like BDSM with him.

Deciding that having dinner would be safer, she said, "That, um, wouldn't be nice."

"What wouldn't?"

"Canceling dinner, especially if they went out of their way to, you know, fit us in."

After a beat, he released her chin. "Okay, pet."

The name's Kimani!

But she kept silent.

He guided her to the door, holding it open for her. They took the elevator down to the garage and got into his Porsche.

"No Wong or Bataar tonight?" she asked, half wishing to have the relative safety of a third person.

"I'm sure Bataar is around somewhere," he said.

As they pulled out of the garage and onto the street, she noticed a car pull up behind them.

"There he is," Ben said, looking into the rearview mirror.

"So he's like your bodyguard."

"Yeah. My dad hired him. I offered Bataar double to go on my payroll, but I'm pretty sure he's still working for my dad."

"You don't sound pleased."

"My dad's paranoid. But it's not like I'm a celebrity or star athlete. No one's going to mob me."

"You mean you're not Hong Kong's most sought-after bachelor?" she couldn't resist teasing.

"I keep a low profile."

"What about kidnapping?"

"I can take care of myself."

"No one's invincible."

"You worried about me, pet?"

She scrunched up her face, wanting to blurt out "hell no" as if she were a child being asked if they liked to eat Brussels sprouts.

"I'd be more worried for the people you're with," she retorted.

"Why is that?"

"Because you have a sadistic streak."

"And you're masochistic. It works out, so

what's the problem?"

"I'm not—well, there's probably a bit of masochism in everyone. Even you."

"Sure."

His answer surprised her. She hadn't expected a guy like him to admit it.

"So, does that mean I get to use the flogger on you?" she asked.

"Nice try. I'm not a switch anymore."

"But you were?"

"When I first started out with BDSM. I trained with a Mistress."

She tried to imagine Ben as the submissive. It didn't feel right. But it was hot picturing his strong, masculine body straining beneath the flogger.

"When did you get into BDSM?"

"After I was done with the gang, I looked for other outlets, other ways to piss off my dad. Passive-aggressive shit that took years to grow out of."

"So you've resolved your daddy issues?"

"I don't know if resolved is the right word, but I've learned to live with it. When did you get into BDSM?"

She didn't know what to say. She couldn't remember if she had lied about it already.

"Fairly recently," she answered.

"How recent?"

Like today.

"I'm actually new to it."

"What do you mean you're new to it?"

"I exaggerated all my answers on the Scarlet Auction questionnaire because I didn't want to give anyone a reason not to bid on me."

"So you lied."

Her mouth went dry. Maybe she shouldn't have been honest.

The streetlight had turned red, allowing him to stop the car and pin her with a stare. "There anything else you want to tell me, pet?"

CHAPTER EIGHTEEN

She looked so damn pretty, Ben almost didn't know what to do with himself. He wanted to think that she had added the makeup for him, a sign that maybe she didn't hate his guts after what he had done to her.

The light turned green, so he turned his attention to shifting gears. He wasn't going to push it with Kimani, not until he had a better handle on how she felt about what had happened.

"Nice move," she commented when he changed lanes, slipping around two slow-moving cars.

"I used to want to be a race car driver," he said.

"To piss your dad off?"

"Partly, but I like driving. Don't get to do much of it anymore." With a rare expanse of open road, he kicked the car into higher gear. "What did you want to be?"

"When I was a kid, I wanted to be a police officer. There aren't many female cops, let alone cops of color. Then I got into basketball and wanted to play in the WNBA."

"You said you did a journalism internship

after graduating Stanford. You still interested in that field of work?"

"Yes and no. The work is interesting."

"What about it appeals to you?"

"Knowledge is power, and journalism is about giving people the power through knowledge and the dissemination of information. Making the world a smaller place so that people can connect and relate with what is happening, whether it's next door or halfway around the globe."

"That sounds very worthwhile. So why not pursue a career in journalism?"

"Oh, um, there's not a lot of jobs anymore, especially in print media. I like to write. You can fit more information into one minute of reading than you can one minute of talking in front of a camera."

"So your dream job would be working for a newspaper?"

"...Yes."

"Any paper in particular?"

She smiled, and her eyes brightened. It was devastating.

"*Washington Post. New York Times.*"

"So if the jobs are few and far between, how does someone like you land a job?"

"Try to get an internship that turns into something. It didn't for me.

"Anything else you can do?"

"Work for free. Freelance."

"You doing any of that?"

"This is talk that people on a date would have," she deflected.

"You got a problem with that?"

"Yes. I don't want it to feel like a date."

He couldn't help himself. "Why not?"

"Because we're not on a date. We're just doing dinner in between sex."

That's how he saw it as well. Only he rarely bothered taking women to dinner. It was too much of a dog-and-pony show when both parties knew the end goal was sex. But for some reason, he wanted to take Kimani to dinner. Even though he was seriously considering giving her back to Jake. She wasn't good for him, and he didn't like her poking around his family affairs. He didn't care if he ended up in the paper in connection with the Scarlet Auction. Jason probably wouldn't care either, but Jason's dad would be livid. He would scold Jason for bringing shame upon the family honor, and Jason didn't need more pressure.

He could try to pay her off, ut he doubted money would motivate her. The way she talked, journalism was about serving a greater good. He would have to figure out another way to do a "catch and kill."

"Sex and extortion," she amended.

"Why didn't you just tell me that what you know was confidential?"

"Would that have stopped you earlier?"

He hesitated. "Maybe. Because Uncle Gordon is running for mayor, this development is the most important project for us. The numbers have to work—we're not the only ones financing this—but it's got to be good for Uncle Gordon, too."

"And the City of Oakland."

"Of course."

"Well, not all developers, maybe not even a majority, care about the community. They're in it to make a buck and then they're on to the next project."

"That's not how we work."

"There's a reason developers don't have a good rep."

"I won't say there aren't a lot of bad eggs: developers that skimp on building materials and aesthetics, developers that try to squeeze every last concession out of the city, developers that play dirty and purchase politicians. But don't paint us as all bad. That would be stereotyping."

"How many good developers versus bad developers can you name?"

"How many Smart Cars did we drive by?"

"What does that have to do with developers?"

"Humor me."

"None, I think."

"Now, when we get to the restaurant, tell me how many Smart Cars we've driven by."

"Okay. Oh, there's one."

By the time they got to the restaurant, she had seen three.

"What you look for, you'll usually find," he told her as he handed the car keys to the valet. "When the media reports a story about a bad developer, the public is primed to seek corroboration, further proof of what they know."

"That's a good thing. Are you suggesting we shouldn't report the bad stuff?"

Seeing one of the valet's gaze linger upon her, he wrapped an arm about her waist and pulled her closer. "Not at all. But there's not enough good stuff reported."

"Okay, it's not ideal that fear, greed and the darker side of humanity sells more papers. We're just giving readers what they want."

"Then how are you truly empowering them? How can you change the world for the better if they're only getting part of the picture?"

"It would be better if the media didn't have to worry about making ends meet. Then they would be more free to report what they believe is more valuable instead of what will sell more papers."

"And how would you accomplish that?"

"My first thought was that media outlets could be government sponsored, but then it would be at the whim of politics, whoever was in office or in control of Congress and funding."

She knit her brows in further thought, looking very cute that way.

"Mr. Lee, how do you do?" greeted the hostess before taking their coats and leading them up the stairs to the private patio set up with a table for two.

He pulled a chair out for Kimani.

"Wow," she exhaled as she took in the view of the ocean to one side and the red gleam of the Golden Gate Bridge to the other.

It would have been nice to have an outdoor patio but the ocean breeze could often be chilly.

"You dine here often?" she asked.

Usually only on special occasions, he realized. Tonight was an exception.

Or was it?

"I don't dine out often," he replied as a server brought them sake and poured the wine into small porcelain cups.

"Really?"

"You sound surprised."

"I guess...if you can afford to, why not?"

"It takes too much time out of one's day. And I like to keep my diet simple."

"I like the noodle place in Chinatown. And I'll never pass up good soul food. Do they have soul food in Hong Kong or Beijing?"

"Unless you consider KFC soul food, I haven't come across any."

She laughed. "I remember driving through central California with friends, and we all had a craving for soul food. We ended up at a KFC."

"This dinner will be different from fried

chicken."

The first appetizer was clam with monkfish and a soft-boiled egg. Kimani picked up the chopsticks, but the way she held them made it difficult to pick up the clam. He pulled his chair around.

"You'll get more leverage if you hold one of the sticks at an angle," he said, demonstrating by picking up a single piece of diced green onion.

She gave it a try. It was better but not sufficient. He took the chopsticks out of her hands and repositioned them in her fingers.

"You really only need to move the top stick," he explained. "The bottom one acts as a base, an anchor."

He could smell the fragrance of the bath bomb on her. Her skin felt incredibly smooth. After releasing her hand, he caressed the length of her forearm. Her sharp inhale and reaction to his closeness instantly roused his blood.

What had he been thinking, taking her here? The next few hours were going to be torture if all he wanted to do was run his hands over her body.

She successfully picked up the clam and smiled. "No one ever taught me the right way to use chopsticks."

A second later, she dropped the clam.

"Guess it takes practice," she muttered, making another attempt.

He had fun watching her work the chopsticks. By the time the second appetizer came, she was starting to get the hang of the utensils. When she picked up a single garden pea after many studious attempts and looked up at him with a wide smile, her eyes shining with triumph, he shared in her delight.

"I've never had Japanese food like this before," she said after the soup with bamboo and Wakame seaweed was followed by sashimi with snow crab. "To be honest, the first time I tried sushi, I wasn't a fan."

"I wasn't either. Most of my family shy away from it, partly because my grandfather refused to touch anything Japanese."

"Why is that?"

"The Rape of Nanjing during World War II. The Chinese government estimates that over three hundred thousand civilians were raped and killed by the Imperial Japanese Army."

"That's harsh."

"My grandfather refused to drive Japanese cars, eat Japanese food, or even use an electronic device if it was made by a Japanese company."

"You don't feel the same way?"

"I don't fault my grandfather. I can't imagine what it would be like to live through mass murder and mass rape. But it doesn't serve subsequent generations. At some point, you have to move on."

"True that. I remember having a lot of discussions at Stanford about whether or not slavery is forgivable."

"Is it?"

"I think it's a personal decision. Some people worry that forgiving means condoning the travesty, and moving on means forgetting. We shouldn't ever forget, but my father used to say that forgiveness is really about freeing yourself."

"Sounds like a wise man."

"Yeah, I probably should listen to him more."

The chef came to check on them, but Ben kept the conversation short. If there was a chance he would return her to Jake, he wanted to max every minute with her.

The next few courses consisted of charcoal-grilled salmon, squid garnished with roe and seasonal vegetables, and a hot pot of Japanese duck dumplings. Each course was paired with its own sake. Although sake usually had a low proof, he could see it having an effect on Kimani, who excused herself to go to the ladies' room.

He was glad that she had appeared at ease throughout the dinner. Save for the moment when he had pulled his chair to hers to show her the proper way to hold chopsticks. So it would seem she didn't hate his guts. But even though she had admitted she'd exaggerated her answers to the BDSM questionnaire, he didn't have any plans on going easy with her punishment.

A waiter came by and refilled his sake cup.

And after he punished her, then what? Would he give her back to Jake before his time was up? He would need some assurances that Jake would treat her properly. Maybe he would make that a condition if Jake wanted to keep the full two hundred thousand.

Problem was, Ben didn't think he could be in the same room with Kimani without wanting to claim her for his own. He'd have to quit the cabin.

His mobile rang.

It was Jake.

CHAPTER NINETEEN

"**A**re you the one having dinner with Benji Lee?" the middle-aged Asian woman in the restroom asked.

"Why do you ask?" Kimani returned as she washed her hands.

"Just curious. I tried to set him up with my niece, but my family back in China told me not to bother. Seems Benji has a lot of different girlfriends. I thought maybe you were the flavor of the week."

Kimani flushed. "Hardly. We're not on a date."

The woman raised her heavily tweezed brows. "Oh? It's kind of a romantic setting up there on the private patio."

"He felt like having kesiki, so here we are."

"You mean kaiseki. This restaurant is renowned for that type of food."

Kimani bit back a retort that she didn't care so much about the food as long as the sex with Ben was good. Instead, she smiled and said, "Good to know. And I should probably share with you that Ben hates being called Benji by anyone other than his family."

Leaving the restroom, she returned to the patio and saw that Ben was on his cell, standing near the glass wall.

"If I decide to give her back to you, it's not going to be tonight," Ben was saying, his back to her. "What do you mean, you're bored with Claire? Use your fuckin' imagination. ... No, I'm not interested in swapping. And you told me it's against the contract terms to loan out your subs.... I told you we can talk about it tomorrow."

Hanging up, Ben shook his head.

"That sounded like Jake," she said.

He turned around. "Yeah."

He held the seat out for her. Sitting down, she saw that dessert, a strawberry sherry mousse topped with citrus sorbet, had been set.

"Sounds like he wants you to give me back?" she inquired.

Ben's face darkened as he took his seat. "Something like that."

"Are you?"

He hesitated before replying, "I haven't made up my mind."

Shit.

She stared at her dessert, but as pretty as it looked, she had lost interest in eating. "So you're considering it."

"According to the contract he signed with the Scarlet Auction, any third-party involvement requires prior authorization from the Scarlet Auction."

"And you're a stickler for the rules?"

"I don't give a fuck about the Scarlet Auction."

"Then why bring up the contract?"

He pressed his lips into a line. "Look, I know you don't like Jake, but I'm sure something can be worked out."

"No, thank you. I don't want to work anything out with that racist creep."

"Who did you think you were going to end up with, selling yourself through the Scarlet Auction? Prince Charming?"

"No, that's Claire's fairy tale."

"You can always walk away."

The more he talked, the more it sounded like he was going to give her back to Jake. Her earlier anger returned twofold, in part because she was upset with herself. She should have known better than to trust he could have her interest. She should have walked out that door when she'd had the chance.

"But then I don't get the money, and I'm out that ridiculous processing fee," she replied.

"I'll reimburse you the processing fee, plus whatever you would have earned."

"I don't want your money!"

He was taken aback.

She reconsidered what she ought to have said if she'd actually participated in the Scarlet Auction for monetary reasons. "I mean, it's not fair for you to have to pay."

"Then finish the week with Jake. There's

only a few days left."

"Are you going to be there?"

"No."

Great. Without Ben there to protect her, who knew what Jake might do. But how was she going to finish her story if she quit? And she needed more evidence if there was any chance of bringing charges against Jake.

"I don't trust Jake," she said firmly.

"Then don't finish the week with him. I told you I could compensate you. And take all the stuff that Beth bought. It's yours to do whatever you want. There's easily ten thousand dollars' worth."

"I don't need ten thousand dollars' worth of clothing."

He raised his brows. "So now you're no longer desperate for money?"

Damn. In her agitation, she kept losing focus of the persona she was pretending to portray.

"I'm not a charity case," she grumbled.

"You'd rather sell yourself for sex than accept charity."

Feeling stupid and lacking a clever response, she said, "Don't patronize me."

A waiter came by and asked if they would like tea or coffee. Kimani shook her head. Sensing tension in the air, the waiter made a quick departure.

She blew out her breath. "Great. He

probably thinks we're having a lovers' quarrel."

"You shouldn't care so much what other people think."

"And maybe you should care a little more."

He narrowed his eyes. "All right. You don't want him thinking we're having a lovers' quarrel, then come over here."

She balked, too angry to want to do anything he asked—demanded, rather. "I wasn't saying that I— I was just speculating what the waiter might be thinking."

"*Now*, pet."

She bristled, not having heard him speak quite so harshly before. She didn't want to follow his orders if he was planning to give her back to Jake—and after all the shit she had put up with!

"Don't make me reach over the table to drag you over here," he warned. "You wouldn't want sake to spill all over that pretty dress."

Her cheeks burned. She didn't doubt he would risk making a scene just to get what he wanted. Stiffly, she got out of her chair and walked over. He pulled her onto his lap. She ground her teeth, but the instant her derriere touched his thigh, other emotions flared within her.

"Try the dessert," he said, spooning some of the mousse and sorbet topped with perfectly cut fruit.

"I'm full," she said, too vexed to think of what to say or how she could exit the situation she had created from a small remark about the waiter.

He held the spoon in front of her. "Try it."

Hating that she felt like she had no choice but to comply, she parted her lips and allowed him to feed her. The sorbet melted on her tongue, filling her mouth with brightness. The dessert was flavorful but without the heaviness of most American desserts. If she wasn't so upset, she would have finished off the dessert.

Ben wiped a drop of the mousse from the corner of her lips into her mouth, pushing his thumb inside. Knowing what he wanted, and hating him more for it, she licked his thumb. When he didn't withdraw, she sucked on it.

"That's a good pet."

She was tempted to bite his thumb, but then she might tick him off so much he could decide to fly her back to Jake tonight.

"Now take off your panties."

"Here?" she exclaimed.

"And now."

She glanced around to see if anyone was coming but still hesitated.

He reached beneath her dress and grabbed the boyshorts. "You want me to rip them off you?"

"No! I've got it."

Fuming, she wriggled them down to the hem of her dress, took another look around, then slid them the rest of the way off her legs. He took

170

them and held them up for assessment. She tried to snatch them back before anyone walked in on them, but he held the panties out of reach. He balled the undergarment and stuck it in his pant pocket. She wasn't going to get the underwear back anytime soon.

"You want the rest of your dessert?" he asked.

"I'm good," she said through clenched teeth.

"Then we can wrap this dinner up and head back to begin your punishment."

*****

The drive back to Ben's place was silent and awkward. Kimani was still upset about having to remain on his lap while the servers cleared dessert and brought the check. At least he hadn't done anything else, like feeling her up. But just knowing he could and he might had set her on edge. And she had yet to come up with a way to convince him not to return her to Jake.

Escape while you can, Kimani.

She closed her eyes, trying to relax enough to think straight. But it wasn't easy. He had said she could come up with her own punishment, but if he didn't like her ideas, he would add his punishment to hers.

"So what's it going to be?" he asked, tossing his keys onto the kitchen counter when they were back in his penthouse.

"You want me to go through a punishment with you, only to have you throw me back to Jake?" she asked.

"You're still mine for tonight, pet."

"That supposed to make me feel better?"

His frown said he didn't give a shit, but his eyes hinted at guilt. She decided to take a chance on the latter.

"Besides, didn't you put me through enough earlier in the day?"

"That was on the tame side, pet."

Not what she wanted to hear.

"So you're okay with what you did? All that exploitation shit?"

He crossed over to her and grabbed her by the back of her neck, his thumb pressed into the soft spot beneath her jaw. "You came, didn't you?"

Her breath skipped. She tried to swallow. "And that justifies it all?"

"You want out?" He released her and nodded toward the door. "Go right ahead. But if you choose to stay, questionnaire or no questionnaire, you agree to take it all."

She looked to the door.

Go. Run. This might be your last chance.

But she remained rooted to the spot. Walking out that door was probably the smart thing to do. But was it also cowardly? What about the other women?

And if she left now, she'd leave empty-handed. She would have no way of contacting the other women. She only had the full names of Jake, Ben and Jason, and she doubted that reaching out to them would prove helpful. All she had was her own personal account of what she had been through, and she doubted that was enough to make the scoop Sam wanted. She didn't want to have any regrets.

Regrets about the scoop or regrets about leaving Ben?

Really, she should hate the guy's guts. Hate him for tormenting her. Hate him for thinking of returning her to Jake.

Try as she might, she couldn't drum up the hatred. She was plenty angry at him. And herself. For enjoying his twisted pleasure and what he did to her body. But she also enjoyed his company. More than enjoyed. They had connected. She wasn't sure if he felt the same way, but, despite her charade, she felt she could be herself with him. And he challenged her in ways she found exciting. She wanted to stay with him.

Oh, but she didn't want to give him the satisfaction of staying. And she was scared. She had no idea what kind of punishment he had in mind.

"If I stay," she began, "what will happen?"

"You take your punishment."

"Then what? Are you returning me to Jake?"

"We'll see about that."

"That doesn't sound like a good deal for me."

"You take your punishment well, you'll get rewarded. I do have one caveat for the punishment, however."

"What's that?"

"No. Safe. Words."

CHAPTER TWENTY

Her eyes lit up with fear. Then came anger. Ben could imagine the words she wanted to throw at him but had enough restraint and smarts to withhold. He knew women who would rant and rave or call him names. He usually found them immature and lacking in self-control.

He wasn't a gambler, despite gambling's popularity in his culture. But this was a big gamble.

Kimani wasn't as hardcore as her answers to the questionnaire had suggested. How much she had exaggerated, he wasn't sure, but he would find out. He had seen the tentative look she had given the door, seen that she had contemplated going through it. A part of him would be relieved if she did. He wouldn't have to worry about returning her to Jake and making sure the wanker didn't give her a black eye or something like it.

If she stayed, he wanted her complete and total submission. He wanted to know how badly she wanted this. And even how much she might want him.

Leaning against the sofa, he let her think it

over in silence. The seconds passed by slowly, and he found himself on edge. What would she decide? There were upsides to whatever she chose, but did he truly want her to walk out that door?

For several seconds, she glared at him.

"Go on," he said. "Call me a jerk, an asshole."

"I'm looking for a better word."

He couldn't resist a small smile. "Stay or don't. It's your choice, pet."

The wheels were turning in her head. She was trying to find a way to turn things in her favor.

"Going without a safety word requires a lot of trust," she considered aloud. "And I can't say you've inspired a lot of confidence in me."

He acknowledged her point with a nod. "Like I said, I wouldn't trust my sisters with a guy like me. You have your warning."

"How likely are you to return me to Jake?"

"I really can't say."

"If I take my punishment well, will you reconsider letting Jake have me back?"

"Maybe."

She should take his offer to compensate her and walk out the door. That would be the wise thing to do. But something compelled her otherwise, and he didn't think it was all him.

She was quiet for several minutes more before saying softly, "I'll stay."

He closed his eyes and let out the breath he hadn't realized he'd been holding.

"No safe words," he reminded her.

"Yes, Master."

He nearly groaned. The word Master sounded so bloody sweet on her tongue. He swept her off her feet and, throwing her over his shoulder, walked down the hall to his playroom. He wanted to get the punishment underway before she changed her mind.

Once in the playroom, he set her down.

"Strip," he told her.

Without protest, she untied the top of the halter and slid it down her body.

Fuck.

He adjusted himself.

"Turn around," he commanded.

She did as told, giving him a view of her backside. Her high heels caused her arse to protrude nicely and the buttocks to tighten. He would definitely be taking a piece of that tonight.

"Feel yourself up."

She turned back around and grabbed her breasts.

"Nice and slow," he directed.

She dug her fingers into the pliant flesh and rolled the orbs over her chest.

"Now play with your nipples."

She tugged at one lightly. Seeing the delicious bud harden, he licked his lips. He drank in the sight of her body, every inch—from her shoulders and collarbones to the chocolate-colored areolas, the subtle indent down her midsection, her belly button, the swell of her hips, the curls at her mound, the length of her legs.

"Play with yourself."

Dropping a hand, she slid her fingers between her thighs.

Feeling the heat, Ben removed his blazer. "What did you come up for your punishment?"

Her gaze lowered briefly. "You could spank me."

"With what?"

"Your hand."

"Anything else?"

She glanced around at the many implements he owned. "The, um, paddle."

He looked at the various paddles, one with holes, one without, one with hearts, and another with the word "slut."

"Which one?"

"The one with holes?"

"Good choice."

His response seemed to startle her. She was second-guessing herself. In case she didn't know, he explained, "The holes allow the paddle to move through the air faster. What else besides a paddling?"

"The cage. You could leave me in one of those."

"Overnight?"

She frowned, but maybe she thought it would be safer in the cage than out, because she replied, "If you wish, Master."

"And then what?"

"Then you could tie me up in shibari."

He nodded. That had made his list as well. "And what should we do when you're all tied up?"

She met his gaze. "You could fuck me, Master."

He was tempted to do just that right now. Flip her over the back of the nearest chair and drive himself into that sweet, sweet cunt.

"Is that it?" he asked.

"And I could give you lots and lots of blow jobs."

He went to stand before her. He cradled a few of her braids in his hand. "With most of my subs, blow jobs are a reward, not a punishment, given after they're begging for my cock."

"You want me to beg, Master? I'll beg."

Her frequent address of him as "Master" surprised him, but he liked it. "Anything else you want to add to your punishment, pet?"

"Do you like it?"

"It's a decent punishment. I think your ideas are good ones."

She let out a soft breath.

"But I do want to mix it up with a few ideas of my own."

Her relief turned to alarm. "Like what?"

He passed his fingers over the area of her collar and between her breasts. "You'll see."

Reaching into his pocket, he pulled out her knickers and took a whiff. They smelled of her.

"They're a bit damp," he told her. "As you won't be using any safe words tonight, you can hold on to these."

Taking her by the jaw, he opened her mouth and stuffed the undergarment inside.

"So pretty," he murmured. "Go lay on the bed."

She did as told. He returned with several items, including a short cord of rope that he wrapped around her mouth to secure the knickers in place.

"I'm not going to tie you down," he said, "since you said earlier today that you were going to be a good pet. Spread your legs."

Gingerly, she parted her legs. He eyed the luscious flesh between before putting his thumb to her clit, encouraging it to emerge farther. Taking a narrow tube, he applied lubricant to the edge and fit it over the clit. He attached a small handheld motor to the top of the tube and turned it on, pulling the air out and sucking her clit into the glass. Her lashes fluttered quickly, and her chest heaved up and down. He detached the motor and tapped on the tube. She whimpered.

"On your knees," he instructed.

While she got into position, he went to grab

a spreader bar. He pulled her hands between her legs and cuffed her ankles and wrists into the spreader bar. She looked amazing with her legs spread, her arse in the air, the side of her face pressed into the mattress, red satin adorning her mouth, the glass tube dangling from her clit.

He rubbed a buttock. Such a nice piece of arse. He liked booty that had padding, had never liked scrawny booties or bodies that looked like jailbait. Kimani was the perfect balance of athleticism and feminine suppleness.

He slapped the cheek he caressed. She tensed. The pink and wrinkled hole between her buttocks teased him. He couldn't wait to sink into that naughty opening.

He spanked the other cheek.

"Mmmph," she mumbled.

He spanked her harder, relishing the smacking sound, then went to get the wooden paddle with holes. He kneaded the flesh, preparing it for the first blow.

She grunted into her panty-gag at the first whack, then yelped at the second. The third one made her scream. He saw her squeeze her eyes shut.

"How many do you think you merit?" he asked as he rubbed where he had struck.

She mumbled something that sounded like "I don't know."

"You've done a lot of lying, which you know I

don't care for."

The paddle flew through the air without a sound till it connected with her arse, sending her body forward.

"And I can't help but feel like there's more you're not telling me."

The next whack left more visible imprints of the holes. He allowed them to fade before paddling her again.

"So how many?" he demanded, pulling her head up by the braids.

She blinked once. Twice. Thrice.

"That's it?" he replied. "I don't think so. I'll let you give me another number. If I don't like it, I'm going to double your answer."

She started anew and blinked ten times.

"That's better," he acknowledged. "But not good enough. We're going to go with twenty."

Letting go of her hair, he rubbed her arse, saw her body brace itself, and gave her the first of twenty blows.

"One," he counted.

She made a sound that could have been a wail or could have been a groan. The next strike made her scream. He stopped at five and looked to see her eyes had started to water. She clenched her hands as she took the next several whacks.

"We'll take a break," he said, halfway through her paddling.

Reaching between her legs, he wiggled the

tube still attached to her clit. It stretched so far it could have made for a tiny penis. He broke the seal of the tube to pet her clit. Her body jumped at his touch. He slicked his fingers with his saliva and gently fondled the swollen bud. She gave a muffled squeal. He worked the clit till her cunt juices began dripping.

Now that she was properly aroused, he went back to the paddling.

Her arse blushed a nice rosy pink. After a few more blows, the knuckles of her fingers had turned white and he noticed she was digging her nails into her palms. He paused to plant kisses on her rump.

"Only five more to go, pet."

Her breathing became shallow. He waited to make sure she wasn't hyper-ventilating. When she had calmed, he continued with the rest of the paddling.

By the time he was done, a tear had escaped the corner of her eye.

He rewarded her with more fondling of the clit but stopped short of an orgasm. Surveying her body folded atop the table, he decided she was in the perfect position for bastinado. Setting aside the paddle, he traced the bottom of her foot with his thumb. She shivered.

"This is an especially sensitive part of the body," he noted. "Foot torture is still practiced in some parts of the world. You had given bastinado the max rating. I hope that wasn't one of your exaggerations."

From his pocket, he took out two rubber bands he had grabbed earlier and wrapped them around one foot. He pulled one back and let it snap back into place. The pitch of her scream was the highest he had heard thus far. He caressed the bottom of her foot before snapping both bands. She screamed again.

"Would you prefer to go back to the paddling?" he asked.

She nodded. But he pulled the rubber bands back. After the snap, she emitted another scream. Her body wanted to scramble away, but there was nowhere for her to go.

She mumbled into the knickers. Probably cursing him. But when she didn't stop, he decided to pull the rope down her mouth. She spat out the knickers and tried to work the moisture back into her mouth before speaking.

"Fuck me."

CHAPTER TWENTY-ONE

Kimani could tell it wasn't what he had expected her to say, but she hoped he would take her up on it. Her ass felt battered and bruised, but she hated the sting of the rubber bands. New tears filled her eyes, and her nose had started to run.

"Are you telling me to fuck you so I'll end the bastinado?" he asked.

"Just fuck me," she replied. "Fuck me good and hard, Master."

She had decided that her best chance of being able to stay with him was to give him what he wanted. She had to admit that the fact he might not finish his week with her had wounded her pride. But a part of him still desired her. She could see it, sense it. If she could be the best pet he ever had, he wouldn't want to give her back to Jake.

For a few seconds, she heard nothing—then the sound of him unbuttoning and unzipping his pants. She hoped she had made the right choice. The tip of his cock grazed her clit, reminding her of how much it throbbed and how uber-sensitive it was. She could come so easily...

He rubbed his shaft along her folds a few times before plunging in.

Damn, that feels soooo good.

The sensation was especially heavenly after the hellacious snapping of the rubber bands. She gave a sharp gasp when he gripped her hips and pushed deep into her.

"Good and hard, as requested," he said before another forceful thrust.

He withdrew slowly, his cock stroking the best parts of her pussy. But then he drilled her so hard, her body scooted several inches. He pulled her back and pumped more softly. She moaned. If she could touch her clit, she could send herself over the edge within seconds. She ground herself on his cock, seeking release.

"Someone likes it doggy-style," he remarked.

The snap of the rubber bands stopped her.

Shit! The fucker.

"You're lucky you didn't come because I haven't given you permission yet."

She groaned. "May I come, Master?"

"No."

He then started to bang her so hard, the bed would have moved if it weren't bolted to the ground. Pain took the upper hand as his pelvis slammed into her sore bottom.

What was he trying to do? Drive his dick into her head?

She couldn't decide if bracing or relaxing her body was better. Provided she could do either. She felt capable of nothing—nothing but serving as a receptacle for his furious pounding. He

186

slowed, maybe trying to achieve one of his non-ejaculatory orgasms. She hoped he wasn't trying to prolong his erection.

He reached around her hip and found her clit.

Sweet Jesus.

He worked her clit while gently thrusting.

Yes, yes, yes!

"Permission, Master," she begged. It felt so good maybe it was worth coming, permission or no?

"Not yet, pet."

Then stop doing what you're doing!

"Aaaargh," she moaned, wanting so desperately to come, to have euphoria wipe everything else away, but needing to resist, needing to stop herself from claiming what her body wanted more than air to breathe.

Furious, her body fought her control, creeping closer to the edge of climax.

Must not come...

What if he punished her with more bastinado?

But her arousal didn't care.

To her momentary relief, he started thrusting roughly once more. She cried out when it felt like he was hammering the depths of her womb.

"That hard enough for you, pet?"

"Y-Yes," she said through chattering teeth.

He planted a foot on the bed beside her,

creating a different kind of leverage with which to thrust into her. He grabbed her braids and started banging away. She tried to find the pleasure amidst the discomfort. Occasionally it seemed his cock grazed the bottom of her clit, sending delightful flutters through her groin.

Her scalp smarted from his pulling, and she wanted to collapse so badly, but the bar kept her body in its cramped position.

Needing him to come, she encouraged him. "Yes, use me, Master. Give it to me. You're so—unh—good at—unh—fucking your little slut."

That did it. With a loud grunt, he slammed himself home. He trembled violently against her. His liquid heat filled her pussy. After several more deep thrusts, he slowed to catch his breath. She felt his sweat fall upon her backside and breathed her own sigh of relief.

If she was lucky, he would be done. But Ben wasn't a typical guy.

And she wasn't so lucky.

CHAPTER TWENTY-TWO

A fucking reporter.

Sitting in the living room, Ben shook his head as he listened to the audio file on the USB of Kimani's pen. What else might she have recorded? And who was her intended target? Jake? The Lee family? Everyone involved in the Scarlet Auction?

He should have dropped her as soon as he suspected she was up to something. But he had let his cock do the guiding. And the incredible pounding he had given her almost washed away all other consideration.

As he had hoped, her body had withstood the rough fucking. And he was willing to bet that he could have gotten her to come easily. A part of him wanted to and had considered grabbing a vibrator for her. Instead, after releasing her from the spreader bar, he had bound her arms behind her with rope and attached three little clamps, all linked together by a thin chain, to her nipples and clit. He then had her climb into the shorter cage.

"What's that for?" she had asked when he'd set an empty dish into the cage.

"In case you need to go," he answered.

She had looked horrified.

He had then set a second dish, filled with water, into the cage before locking it shut, telling her, "If you're able to get yourself to come, you have my permission."

Unless she was one of the lucky women who could come through thought alone, she'd have a hard time. Through the webcam, he watched her try to fit a leg between the bars of the cage, probably hoping to rub her clit against a bar, but the space between the bars was too narrow.

"Where's the girl?" asked Bataar when Ben met him at the gym. "She's a cute one."

Ben frowned as he prepared to spar with the large Mongolian. "Back at my place."

Bataar threw the first punch, which Ben ducked. "When are you heading back to the cabin?"

"I haven't decided yet."

They circled one another.

"My research didn't turn up anything else on Jake Whitehurst," Bataar said.

Ben threw a kick, which Bataar defended. "Didn't think it would."

"I did find an ex-girlfriend who called him a prick in one of her Facebook posts."

"And?"

"I thought there would be something more. You know, based on what Kimani had said."

"He's been an asshole to her."

But I'm probably the bigger asshole.

Bataar delivered a low kick, which Ben jumped over.

"She's inclined to think the worst of Jake," he finished.

"Don't trust women's intuitions?" Bataar asked.

"Unbiased, women are more reliable than men. But I'm not sure she's not biased. She's working some angle."

"Angle?"

"Yeah, she's been jerking me around—"

Bataar's strike glanced off the side of his head. Ben shook off the blow. He was losing focus, which was becoming a habit when it came to Kimani.

"How?" asked Bataar.

"She's an undercover reporter."

Ben got his revenge, faking a punch with his left before delivering with his right.

"No shit?" Bataar asked before going low again.

Ben jammed his foot over Bataar's, pinning it to the mat. "She snuck a recording pen into the cabin."

"You on it?"

"Along with Jake and the others."

"She working a story on lecherous guys who buy women for sex?"

"You calling me a lech?"

Bataar grinned. "Sure, boss. You bought her for sex, didn't you?"

Only I didn't have to. It turned out to be a big mistake.

Apparently wanting to make his boss feel better, Bataar added, "Hey, you made a nice purchase. She's—"

Ben didn't let him finish, kicking Bataar in the stomach. Bataar stumbled back.

"Anyway," Bataar said, rubbing his stomach before getting back into position. "What are you going to do about it?"

"Don't know yet. I don't know what she knows, and I don't know her intentions."

He'd tried tormenting truth out of her and that hadn't worked. He wasn't sure he was up to doing it again. She had called it a low blow.

"I've given her plenty of opportunities to tell me the truth."

"You could confront her," Bataar suggested. "Tell her you're onto her game."

He could. He had refrained from doing so in part because he hadn't wanted to scare her off, and he'd thought he could find out what he needed to know in between fucking her brains out.

"Or just let it go if you don't think she has anything to bust you with. You're not likely to cross paths again when you're done with her."

For some reason, the thought rattled him. Bataar went low. Ben avoided the first kick, but Bataar spun around and swept his foot behind Ben, knocking him off balance. He fell to the

192

mat.

"Or maybe you don't plan to be done with her?"

Ben narrowed his eyes and hopped back up. "Of course I'm going to be done with her. Why do you think I wouldn't be?"

"Because I've never knocked you off your feet before. And it was almost too easy."

"I was distracted—thinking too much."

"Sure, boss."

The sparring ended less satisfactorily than Ben had wanted. Towards the end, Bataar had pinned him to the mat, a rare occurrence. Ben had hoped the sparring would take his mind off Kimani. Instead, she had barely left his mind.

Back at his place, he drew in a deep breath. He had opted not to take a shower at the gym because he wanted to get to Kimani and see how she was doing in person. He found her lying on her back with her knees in the air. He walked up to the cage and dropped his sweats. His cock had stiffened on the drive back as he'd contemplated the rest of her punishment.

He pointed his hard-on at her. She got to her knees. He fit his cock in between the bars of the cage. She took it into her mouth.

So bloody good.

She did her best to go and up down his shaft without the aid of her hands. Reaching through the cage, he fisted his hand into her braids and pushed her against his crotch. She started gagging, so he pulled back.

When presented with the opportunity to walk out the door without losing out on the money she could have earned from the Scarlet Auction, she had opted to stay. As much as he wanted to think it was because of him, it was because she had more work to do for her undercover project. That was what motivated her. Not money. Not him.

Upset, he shoved her back onto his cock, forcing her to deep throat him. He kept her there for several seconds, her nose tickling his pubes, before pulling her off him. She started to cough.

He could offer to go light on her punishment if she told him everything, but he wouldn't be able to confirm whether or not she withheld anything. He went through all that she might have heard or recorded and wondered if she had tried to access his email the times she'd had his mobile. But his email required a password.

"Make me come in five minutes if you don't want more bastinado," he said.

He released her hair, making her do all the work. She went to town on his cock, slurping and sucking with vigor. He pulled off his tank and closed his eyes, enjoying every amazing second. Deciding to toy with her a little, he backed away. She had to press her face to the bars of the cage to get at his cock.

"Please, Master, can I have your cock?" she begged. "I want it so bad. You taste soooo good.

I've got to have your cock."

Even though he knew she was acting the part, his vanity smiled. She looked almost like a baby bird waiting to be fed. Holding the base of his cock, he guided it into her eager mouth. She sucked him till her cheeks caved inward. He helped her by fisting his hand into her hair once more, pushing and pulling. She gagged from time to time, drooling a little at the corners of her lips.

He bucked his hips. She couldn't quite keep up, but he was too close to coming.

His cum blasted from him, overflowing her mouth as she tried to come off him to prevent his semen from accidentally shooting down the wrong pipe. Ecstasy quivered from his head to his toes.

"Every drop, pet," he said as the last of his cum spurted from him.

She swallowed what she could and tried to lick what had come out of her mouth as well as his shaft, smearing some of his seed on the sides of her face in her effort. She couldn't reach the drops on her thighs, so he scooped them up with his finger and had her clean off his digit.

"Um," she said when she was done.

She was fucking amazing.

And in that moment, there was no fucking way he was returning her to Jake.

CHAPTER TWENTY-THREE

Her cheeks were sore from the blow job, her arms were sore from being bound behind her for so long, but making him come had only aroused her further. Kimani had tried her best to get herself off, but the confines of the cage provided her nothing. The clip on her clit drew all her attention there, mocking her with its consistent kiss of her pleasure bud. She had tried rubbing her legs together, hoping that the movement of the clip would be enough to send her into orgasm, but she had only succeeded in accidentally disengaging the clip.

"That was bloody great," Ben breathed.

"Thank you for your cock, Master," she said, glad that she was no longer alone.

He hadn't been gone for more than an hour and a half, but the time had passed so slowly. During that time, she vacillated from anger to resentment, from frustration to longing, from betrayal to arousal. Never before had she felt so many conflicting emotions at once, nor felt so lost. It was crazy of her to agree to go into a session of BDSM with no safe words. After all that Ben had done to her, how could she trust him?

Strangely, she did. And she couldn't say why. Just some gut feeling deep down. Her mind couldn't rationalize it. She could keep telling herself that what she did was about finding a way to return safely back to the cabin, in Ben's protection, and keeping the scoop alive. That what she did had nothing to do with him.

But it wouldn't be true.

She wanted more of him. And she wanted to be his, his in whatever ways he would have her,

Her gaze met his through the bars, and she wished she knew what was he thinking. The look he gave her made her hopeful that maybe he was having second thoughts about returning her to Jake.

He pulled up his sweats, then opened the cage and helped her out. He removed the clips from her nipples and massaged a breast. Lowering his head, he captured a nipple in his mouth. She gasped loudly. Her nipple was so tender from the clip, she wasn't sure if she wanted the attention. But then his hand was between her thighs, and she decided she would suffer anything if he would make her come.

He bit and sucked her nipple while his fondling made her whimper. Moving off her nipple, he kissed his way up to her lips. When his mouth claimed hers, she couldn't have been happier. She loved the way he kissed her. Always deliberate. Whether all-consuming or laser focused, his kisses invigorated even while they made her insides melt.

"Why'd you decide to stay?" he murmured against her lips.

"I don't know. I hope I don't live to regret it." She pulled back to look into his eyes. "Will I?"

"It depends."

"On what?"

He searched her eyes as much as she searched his. "Why don't you tell me the reason you're here."

"Because...oooh."

His fingers had curled inside her, stroking the nerves there.

"I really don't know," she whimpered.

"I think you do."

"Because I agreed to do a week."

"That's a bullshit answer."

Pleasure fluttered through her with his caressing.

"What do you want me to say then?" she said. "You. You're the reason, Master. I can't get enough of you."

To her surprise, he seemed upset by that. Withdrawing his fingers, he turned her around and undid the rope binding her arms.

Had she set him off? She had thought he would like her answer!

He retied the rope, binding her wrists in front of her this time. She liked the look of the rope against her skin. He pulled her wrists up and bent her arms so that her hands rested behind her head. He then wrapped the rope across her upper arms and face, fitting the rope between her lips to form a gag.

"Don't patronize me with falsehoods," he told her when he was done.

Retrieving more rope, he bound her chest next, putting her breasts in a cage of rope, which he then looped through rings dangling from the ceiling. After securing the top of her body, he wrapped another cord of rope about the top of her thigh. He looped the rope though another ring and hoisted her leg into the air. He secured the end of the rope around her lower thigh before repeating the process on the other leg.

When he was done, she was suspended in the air in a cradle of rope.

He went to the sideboard. She hoped he came back with the SONA or Womanizer. But what he held was a wand that came to a point.

Turning it on, he touched the tip to her underarm.

Her body jerked at the zap of electricity. Oh no. This wasn't good.

He touched the wand to her inner thigh.

Shit!

The wand zapped her breast next. She screamed into her rope gag.

She braced herself before each zap, yelping and crying each time the intense static sparked against her body. It even sounded as bad as it felt. He touched the zapper to her rib, her butt, then back to her arms and legs. Even though she had nowhere to go, her body wriggled and writhed. When he was done raining the electricity upon her, she was panting, praying for it to be over. He gave her one final zap on the underside of her foot before putting it away.

Motherfucker!

If she could kill him right now, she would seriously consider doing it.

Except that he had returned with a magic wand. Turning it on, he put it to her clit and pussy. Delicious vibrations made her forget the bite of the zapper. He cradled the wand at her clit while he finger-fucked her with the same hand. It was wonderful. Fan-fucking-tastic.

Please let me come. Please don't let it be a setup for orgasm denial.

Part of her didn't want to give in to the beautiful sensations for fear that he would leave her bereft.

"Permission to come," she said through her gag, hoping he understood her.

He didn't respond.

"Please," she begged as her body rode the wave higher. "*Please.*"

Oh no. She was going to come no matter what.

"Please, please, please!"

"Come," he ordered.

And with that, her body went into

200

convulsions. Rapture exploded, blossoming to her head, out through her body. She was and wasn't in her body, occupying some other dimension of pleasure. Of the most amazing, most decadent bliss. When he pulled out his fingers, wetness streamed from her. She almost sobbed from the relief and joy of it all.

CHAPTER TWENTY-FOUR

As her head had no support, Ben released her from the suspension bondage. If he knew Kimani to be more experienced in rope bondage, he would have left her tied up longer. He once had a Japanese sub who could balance herself from a single-point suspension wrapped about her hips.

After unwrapping all the rope, he carried her to the bed. She was tired, but he was going to wrest another orgasm out of her before he was done. He settled himself between her legs and licked her folds. Her scent sent the blood coursing to his groin.

She purred softly as his tongue worked her clit. He feasted on her till her wetness dripped down onto the bed and she dug her hands into the bedsheet. As he continued the cunnilingus, he inserted his fingers into her sodden heat and drew out the moisture to transfer it to her anus.

"Wait!" she gasped when he put a digit to her puckered opening.

"Did you forget you told me to fuck your arse?"

"I did?"

"You said something along the lines of how

nice and tight your arse is, ready to be stretched by your Master. And you're right: I did want your arse the instant I saw it."

"Oh," was all she said, but she remembered.

"Don't worry," he soothed. "You liked it before, didn't you?"

"Yeah, but it hurt the first time I tried it."

"I'm willing to bet you're going to be a fan."

"I hope so."

He was rather touched that she was willing to give it a try with him. He flipped her over onto her stomach and pulled a pillow beneath her to prop her arse in the air, then went to grab some lubricant and a vibrator. Turning on the vibrator, he placed it in her hand and had her hold it to her clit. After kicking off his sweatpants, he rubbed the lube all over his cock. His balls were boiling with excitement. Her arse was going to be the *pièce de résistance.*

Settling behind her, he pressed the tip of his cock to her opening. The small hole resisted when he pushed.

"Relax," he said, rubbing her lower back and massaging her buttocks with his free hand.

Holding himself, he allowed the vibrator to heat up her arousal before he pressed the head of his cock into her. His breath caught as he watched her arse swallow the crown. She gave a shaky gasp when the head popped into her fully.

The tightness was more marvelous than he had thought possible. Her rectum contracted, trying to push out the unnatural intrusion, which only made it feel more amazing. He poured more lube onto his cock before sinking farther.

"Oh, Jesus," she groaned. "May I come?"

"Anytime, pet."

She pressed vibrator against herself and came with a cry. The contractions rippled over his cock. He wanted so badly to shove his entire length into her, but he waited till he thought she was ready. He slid more of himself into her.

"Oh, my God, my God," she murmured.

Little by little, he managed to bury his entire shaft inside her arse. The feel of her buttocks against his pelvis was beautiful. He could stay here forever.

Reaching beneath her, he switched the vibrator up a notch. When she started to moan again, he slowly withdrew his cock and slowly pushed back in. Maybe one of these days he would be able to thrust into her with all his strength. He found himself eager for that day.

"You're going to come for me again, pet," he told her.

"Un-hunh," she murmured.

She flexed about his cock, threatening his forbearance, but he paced himself until he sensed her next climax nearing. He dared to thrust quicker and a little harder. It seemed she got louder.

He could fuck her arse all day long, he

decided. How could he have considered giving her back to Jake? There was no way he was going to let another man near an arse as fine as this.

Her words became incoherent and built into a scream as her orgasm broke over her, sending her into spasms. Unable to resist any further, he pumped himself deep until he unloaded into her, draining himself into the most exquisite rapture to ever take hold of his body.

How the hell was he going to be able to give this up?

*****

Sometime in the middle of the night, Ben moved Kimani into his bedroom. In the morning, instead of getting out of bed early to do his *tai chi chuan*, he stayed in bed with her, enjoying the soothing sound of her breathing. He had woken with a hard-on and wanted nothing more than to reach over and make love to her, but he let her sleep. She had been through a lot.

The ringing of his mobile caused her to stir. Grabbing his phone, he got out of bed and went into the bathroom, closing the door behind him. The call was from Jason.

"You coming back anytime soon?" his cousin asked.

"Haven't decided. Why?"

"Oh, well, it's Jake. He was doing some erotic

asphyxiation thing on Claire, and she passed out. I thought since you're pretty deep into stuff like that, maybe you could show Jake how it's done."

"Is she okay now?"

"Yeah, yeah, she's totally fine. She's with the other women. They're doing each other's nails. But I think she's, like, kinda scared."

"We'll be back today. Text me if Jake tries anything else."

Shit. After last night, his desire to go back to the cabin had fallen to zero.

There was a knock on the door. "Ben?"

He opened the door to find Kimani wrapped in the bedsheet. Given how much time she had spent naked before him, her modesty was quaint.

"Everything okay?" she asked.

"Jake's being stupid," he told her. "We should head back to the cabin today."

"What happened?"

"According to Jason, Jake was fooling around with asphyxiation, and Claire passed out."

"Jesus! Is she okay? Did they call an ambulance?"

"I think she's okay, but we should see for ourselves."

"I'll get dressed right away."

He didn't want her to get dressed. He wanted her to take care of his wood and to drown himself in her magnificence. But he could see she was concerned about Claire.

After taking a quick shower and jacking off to relieve the tension, he got dressed and found Kimani in the living room wearing a skirt and top they had purchased at the Weaverville thrift shop.

"Would it be okay if I gave one of these dresses to Claire?" Kimani asked.

"All the clothes are yours to do with as you want."

While he had Bataar make arrangements for his jet to fly them to Weaverville, he made a quick breakfast of cooked eggs and orange juice for Kimani. A little over an hour later, they were aboard the Embraer Legacy.

"I'm going with this time," Bataar declared, settling into a seat.

"You are? Great!" Kimani exclaimed.

Ben wasn't as thrilled. He had hoped that he could get Kimani to straddle him and ride his cock.

But he allowed Bataar to come. Maybe Jake was a looser cannon than he had thought. Kimani had been right. Whether willfully or through idiocy, Jake could hurt someone.

Shortly after they were in the air, Kimani got up to use the bathroom. Ben decided to follow her.

"What are you—" she started when he closed the bathroom door behind him.

He responded by stepping into her till she backed up against the counter, wrapping his hand around the back of her neck, and pulling her into a voracious kiss. She resisted for the first few seconds but eventually gave in. He smothered her lips with his mouth. The taste of her was finer than the fare at any Michelin star restaurant.

After several minutes of devouring her mouth, he reached between her thighs.

At that, she tried to separate from him.

"You're not trying to— Bataar is out there," she objected.

"He's sitting in the front of the plane," he replied, shoving his hand where it wanted to be. "You a member of the mile-high club?"

"No!" She tried to push his hand away.

"You're going to be."

"The flight's not even that long!"

"Don't worry. I'll have you coming in twenty minutes or less."

She scowled at his stubbornness but made no further objections for the time being. Her skirt was inconveniently long, so he yanked it down her hips, along with her underwear. He kissed the parts he had bared: her belly, her hips, and, turning her around, her arse. He caressed her rump with his hands while he nipped and bit the lovely half spheres. As he did so, his fingers found her clit.

"I still think..."

But her words turned into a moan. She shivered. He fondled her nub till it became engorged and wetness seeped from her slit. Rising, he undid his shorts and pulled out his cock.

"We shouldn't. We're going to make too much noise."

He recalled how loud she had screamed last night when he'd penetrated her arse.

"You scream all you want, babe. I'll take care of the noise," he told her, positioning his cock below her arse and rubbing it along her pussy lips.

He pushed himself into her. *Bloody marvelous.*

She tried to stifle a groan but cried out when he buried most of his length. He grabbed her wrists and held them together behind her back with one hand. The other he put over her mouth before pulling her the rest of the way onto his shaft.

She protested into his hand, but her words were unintelligible. He thrust at the angle that was best for her pleasure. More of her wet heat engulfed his cock, coaxing him to pound himself into pieces within her. He worked his cock in and out till he felt her body straining towards climax. Then he started bucking his hips a little more forcefully, driving himself deeper.

He kept his hand tightly over her mouth as he fucked her over the bathroom sink. He stared at the mirror, reflecting their bodies joined together. Her eyes were wide, and she breathed heavily through her nose.

"I can't wait to take you in the arse again," he murmured as he smacked his pelvis into her buttocks. "You liked it when I did, didn't you?"

She only grunted.

"Answer me, pet."

"...Mmmmphs."

He took that as a yes and rolled his hips into her. Her lashes fluttered, then her eyes rolled toward the back of her head. She looked so hot.

She made more noises into his hand, eventually becoming one long note as she trembled and bucked against him. He slammed into her harder, faster, pummeling her buttocks with short, fast thrusts till he, too, erupted, pumping his seed into her waiting heat.

"You are fucking amazing," he murmured into her ear before releasing her wrists and dropping his hand from her mouth.

"Oh my God," she exhaled as, legs trembling, she braced herself against the sink.

He replaced his cock and zipped up his shorts. "I'll let you finish going to the bathroom, and don't worry about Bataar. I don't think he heard anything since he's wearing his Beats."

CHAPTER TWENTY-FIVE

Bataar might not have heard anything, but Kimani was sure he was aware that the two of them had been in the bathroom for some twenty minutes. He didn't look her way, however, when she emerged from the bathroom. She took a seat beside Ben.

"So the sex that just happened," she began. "Was that farewell sex?"

Ben fixed his gaze on her, his expression unintelligible. "What do you mean?"

"Are you giving me back to Jake when we reach the cabin?"

He stared at her in for several long seconds. "It's against the terms of the Scarlet Auction. But, no, I'm not giving you back."

She sighed in relief. "Thank you."

"You'd be violating the terms, too, so I'm not sure how that's going to play out for you where the Scarlet Auction is concerned."

"I'll take the consequences if I don't have to deal with Jake."

"What would have happened if I hadn't decided to buy you from him?"

She pursed her lips in thought. "I probably would have called it quits. It's not worth it."

"What's not worth it?"

She sucked in her breath. "The money."

"Just the money?"

"What else would there be?"

He reached into his pocket and pulled out her pen. "This?"

She stared at in disbelief. He had it this whole time?

"You want to tell me about the pen and what makes it so special?" he asked. "I know it doesn't have anything to do with luck."

She swallowed with difficulty. Could he possibly be on to her?

Yes.

She wasn't sure how much he knew, but when she dared to meet his gaze, she saw that she couldn't dismiss him with another lie. She reached for the pen, but he held it out of reach.

"How badly do you want this pen?"

Not knowing what exactly had been recorded, she couldn't say for sure. She replied, "It depends."

"On what?"

Should she tell him? What would happen if she told him the truth?

Various memories came back to her, of him questioning her about graduate school and what career she saw for herself. Had he suspected something all this time? If so, maintaining the lie would only raise his ire.

He wasn't giving her back to Jake. He had a business deal with the guy that might be in jeopardy if he didn't stay in Jake's good graces, but Ben was willing to risk it to keep her. Maybe she owed him the truth, or at least part of it.

He knew her pen was no ordinary pen, so she should probably come clean on that.

"It depends on what's on the recording," she said at last.

He appeared unsurprised, confirming her thought that he knew what the pen was about.

"Nothing criminal. Just eight consenting adults engaged in role-playing."

"You mean when the women were made to act like pets?"

"Yes. You want to tell me why you were recording all of us?"

What if what she said upset him? Would he change his mind about returning her to Jake? She could always leave. Worst case, she wouldn't get her story. And maybe it would take her longer to get a job at a place like the *Tribune*, but it wasn't like her whole future hinged on whether she got the scoop on the Scarlet Auction.

A part of her wanted to tell Ben, too. She was tired of the charade, tired of dancing around his questions. She wanted him to know the truth.

"Do you mind if I use your phone to text someone?" she asked. "Then I'll tell you more."

"Let me guess: you're texting Sam."

She nodded. He did nothing, and for the moment, she thought he would refuse, but he handed her his cell. She typed the following:

This is Kimani. We're heading

back to Jake's cabin in Trinity
County. Will contact you again
when I arrive.

"You want to tell me who Sam really is?" Ben asked after she had returned his phone.

"I'm not in the Scarlet Auction for the money," she said, then took another long deep breath. "I'm working on a— My roommate participated in the Scarlet Auction not too long ago. She got beaten up badly by some creep not unlike Jake. I'm investigating the Scarlet Auction so that what happened to my roommate doesn't happen again."

"Investigating for whom?"

"For the public."

"And Sam?"

"Sam is...someone who can help me. We're thinking of putting together an expose on the questionable practices of the Scarlet Auction."

"I'm not interested in appearing in any expose."

"Oh, we'd change people's names to protect the innocent."

"Is your interest only in the Scarlet Auction?"

"Yes."

"You're not investigating me or my family?"

"My interest is preventing another woman from getting beat up. I swear."

He stared hard at her, as if he were trying to see *into* her. "You're very dedicated to this expose."

"What do you mean?"

"Or is sex with a man you barely know pretty commonplace for you?"

She flushed. "I wasn't planning on having any sex."

"Then why did you?"

"Because..."

Because you came along. You and your—the things you do.

"Because you messed everything up," she finished.

At that, he laughed.

"Seriously," she said. "You've compromised me. I don't know how much of a story I can get out of this now."

"Would you like to be compromised some more?"

Yes, yes, yes!

She scolded herself for being a crazy sex friend. Glancing at Bataar, she saw a faint grin on his lips. Turning back to Ben, she said, "You one of those guys who thinks about sex every seven seconds?"

"When I'm with *you*, pet. The thing is, I don't think you're far off seven seconds yourself, babe."

She turned redder. 'Cause he was right. Right now, if he commanded her to jump his bones, she just might do it. Bataar or no Bataar.

CHAPTER TWENTY-SIX

"Jake took his slut to Weaverville," Vince informed them as Ben and Kimani stepped inside the cabin. "Everyone else is out on the boat."

"I'm going to get myself some water," Kimani said. "You want some?"

Ben nodded, his attention half on Vince, a tall, bulky guy who seemed to serve as security for Jake but also ran errands, like picking up lunch.

"Jake should be back soon," Vince said before leaving the two of them alone in the main room.

While Kimani filled two glasses with water in the kitchen, Ben went out on the deck to take a call from Uncle Gordon.

"Ben, what do you know about the PAC called Oakland Forward?" Uncle Gordon ask.

"It's an independent expenditure chaired by Ezra Rosenstein," Ben answered. "Why do you ask?"

"You didn't see the article?"

"What article?"

"There's an article today in the online edition of the *Tribune*. Nothing major, but I got a call from the FPPC about it."

"What's the FPPC?"

"The Fair Political Practices Commission, a state agency that oversees the laws governing campaigns. I think they're launching an investigation."

Ben was silent for several seconds. "What did they ask?"

"They wanted to know what your involvement with the PAC was, what sort of communications my campaign has had with Oakland Forward. I said I didn't know you were involved with the PAC, and that my campaign has had no contact with Oakland Forward. But the FPPC isn't just going to take my word for it."

"The formation of the PAC was my idea," Ben relayed, "but I handed everything over to Ezra. I'm not involved with it anymore."

"I believe you, but the article raises suspicions."

Ben started to pull up the *Tribune* on his phone. "Let me read the article. I'll call you back."

Sure enough, there was an article on the website for the *Tribune* describing Oakland Forward as the brain child of Benjamin Lee, nephew to mayoral candidate Gordon Lee. Despite the name of the PAC, the article alleged that Oakland Forward was a developer- and business-based committee supporting Gordon Lee for mayor. According to the article, research on the donors to Oakland Forward were a perfect match to the donors of Gordon Lee's campaign.

Just as Ben finished reading the article, he got a call from the pollster Stephens had hired to assess the potential impact Ben and Jason's actions with the Scarlet Auction would have on Uncle Gordon's campaign.

"You asked me about a pro-business committee supporting your uncle," the pollster said. "Is this stuff aboutOakland Forward what you meant?"

"Yeah. Uncle Gordon got a call from the FPPC about it. What's your gut read on this?"

"That it's worse than any sex scandal involving extended family. Even if the FPPC doesn't turn up any wrongdoing by Gordon or his campaign, the *semblance* or possibility of wrongdoing is enough to cost Gordon points."

Ben could feel himself turning several shades darker.

"The public is used to sexual misconduct. You could be a grandfather banging an eighteen-year-old Russian whore and still get elected to high office. But political misdeeds, especially if the candidate himself could be involved, is harder to weather. Now, I can't for say certain without seeing numbers, but you asked for my gut read."

"When can you get numbers?"

"Give me a few days. My callers are still

finishing your first inquiry."

Fuck, Ben swore after hanging up. He stormed inside to find Kimani pulling a pen—the same kind of pen he had asked about on the jet—from a potted plant. She looked up in surprise.

"You swore you were only targeting the Scarlet Auction," he accused.

She furrowed her brow. "That's right."

"Then how do you explain the article on the *Tribune*'s website?"

Her mouth fell open. She did not have the look of someone who didn't know what the hell he was talking about.

"What article?" she asked slowly.

"The article your friend Sam wrote about a PAC supporting my uncle."

Realization flickered in her eyes, evidence that she knew about the article.

"I didn't know about the article," she protested.

"Bull. Shit."

"Look, I, um, I might have been interested—I mean I was open to there being—"

He didn't want to hear any more. He needed air. Fuck. He wasn't sure how Kimani had known about the PAC and his connection to it, but it was all his fault. If he had not been so careless around her. If he hadn't allowed her into his life in the first place. If he had not bought her to begin with.

"I'm going for a drive," he told her.

"Wait!"

But he was too upset for conversation.

"Ben!"

Without looking back, he stalked out of the cabin. Outside, Bataar was standing next to the rental.

"Start the car," Ben ordered.

Bataar complied without a word. Ben hopped in the car.

"Where to, boss?" Bataar asked.

Ben didn't spare the cabin a glance. "For now, head back to the airport."

CHAPTER TWENTY-SEVEN

Kimani was at a loss. She didn't know what article Ben was referring to, but she guessed that Sam had written up something—something that was not to Ben's liking. And she couldn't help but feel responsible. If she had never relayed what she had to Sam, there would be no article for Ben to be upset about.

How was she going to make this right?

She sank down on one of the dining chairs and stared at the two glasses of water on the table. Somehow, after owning up to her part in this, she had to convince him that she hadn't intended to create trouble for him. She desperately wanted to know what was in that article. Had Sam discovered more to write about?

Hearing the front door open, she leaped to her feet, glad that Ben was back so that she could try to explain herself.

But it was Claire who walked in. The young blond looked happy, and she wasn't naked. So Jake had allowed her clothing for a change.

"Oh! Montana, you're back!" she chirped. "I got to go shopping like you did! Not the shopping I was expecting because there's not like a Nordstrom or anything here, but look what Jake bought me."

She showed off a diamond and emerald ring.

"He felt bad for what happened this morning," Claire explained. "This emerald was mined right here in Trinity County. Isn't it gorgeous?"

Kimani was about to agree when she heard a voice that sent her hair crawling.

"Well, look who's back," Jake sneered.

Every nerve was on edge, but she returned his stare. "Ben stepped out, but he'll be back—"

Jake took steps toward her. "Actually, Vince told me he left in his car, right after you guys arrived. Guess he couldn't dump you fast enough."

She wanted to put the width of the dining table between them, but she didn't want him to think that she was scared of him. She did her best to draw herself to her full height and square her shoulders, though his advance made her jumpy.

"Must've gotten bored of black pussy."

He was within arm's reach. Her nerves screamed at her to move away.

"Don't worry. You can suck real cock now," he told her.

"Maybe later," she replied.

He clocked her with a right hook that left her head ringing. Claire screamed but scrambled out of the way.

"Stupid bitch," Jake spat. "You know, this would've all been better if you had been a good little ho and sucked my dick like you were supposed to in the first place."

She saw his next strike coming, but his fist still managed to glance off her head, sending her sprawling to the floor.

"But I'm going to give you a second chance." He unbuckled his belt.

Her brain still felt off balance. She tried to focus on what her next move should be. A quick glance at Claire's stunned face confirmed that there would be little assistance in that department. Therefore, her best bet would be to escape the cabin altogether. She'd rather take her chances in the woods than with Jake. But he blocked her egress.

"What's the matter?" Droplets of his spit landed on her. "Not ready for real cock?"

To Kimani's huge relief, she heard Ben's voice. He had come back!

Jake frowned, visibly upset, but he didn't budge. "Looking for your Chinaman? I'm done with him. He's not welcome here anymore."

She heard Vince's voice, then Ben's response.

"So you better suck my cock good," Jake told her, "or you're going to be one unhappy nigga."

The sounds of a scuffle drew Jake's attention. They heard Vince grunt, followed by the crunch of bones.

Alarmed, Jake ran over to a small sideboard, fished out a key and unlocked the drawer. He pulled out a revolver and slipped in several bullets.

Claire screamed again when she saw the gun.

"Shut up!" he barked at her.

In walked Ben. Kimani's earlier relief had dissipated now that Jake had a gun pointed at him.

Ben's quick glance of the surroundings seemed to take in everything, from Claire to Kimani to Jake.

"Put the gun down," Ben told Jake.

"Where's Vince?"

"He's nursing a broken arm. Now, put the gun down."

Jake's hand was shaking, and Kimani worried that the gun might go off accidentally.

"No," Jake replied. "You just get the hell out of my cabin."

"You going to shoot me if I don't?"

Jake snickered. "Why not? It's self-defense. You're trespassing on my property."

"Fine. I'll leave. But I'm taking Jason and her with me."

Jake looked at Kimani. "She's not going anywhere. She's *my* slut."

"I paid—"

"I don't care what you paid!" Jake's voice had

turned shrill, and the shaking of his hand grew worse. "Just get outta my fuckin' cabin!"

Ben stared at Jake as if doing that alone could get Jake to back down. "You don't want to—"

Kimani launched herself at Jake, shoving his arm into the air while she delivered a body blow, knocking them both to the ground. The gun went off, but the bullet went into the ceiling.

Moving quickly, Ben stomped on Jake's wrist. When Jake let go of the gun, Ben picked it up. Grabbing Jake by the shirtfront, he hauled him to his feet and slammed him up against the wall.

"You stupid fuck," he cursed in Jake's face before throwing him over the table.

Bataar entered, dragging Vince behind him. "Hey, boss, what do you want me to do with him?"

Ben tossed Bataar Jake's gun. "Keep an eye on Dumb and Dumber."

From where he'd landed on the floor, Jake glared at Ben. "The deal with Tyrell Jenkins is off! No way I'm gonna let him go to China after this."

Ben didn't bother replying. Instead, he helped Kimani to her feet. There was so much she wanted to say to him, but he looked away before she could utter a word.

CHAPTER TWENTY-EIGHT

"There," said Marissa as she added the finishing touches of makeup to Kimani's cheek. "Can't see the bruise at all. You're lucky you have dark skin."

"Thanks." Kimani looked at herself in the mirror of their bathroom and saw only the faint shadow of a bruise beneath the concealer and powder. Her cheek was still slightly swollen, and it was sore to the touch. Jake had managed to hit her in the same spot twice, once on their first meeting and again on their last meeting.

That last day at the cabin had been a blur, save for the emotions that still haunted her: fear, dismay, panic, relief, helplessness, despair, and misery. She remembered fearing for her life when Jake had pulled out the gun, then panicking that Jake might shoot Ben. The thought of Ben hurt—or worse—had galvanized her out or her paralysis to take a chance on knocking the gun from Jake.

"I wasn't going to shoot anyone," Jake had protested when everyone else had returned, shocked and confused to find Claire in tears, Kimani holding an ice pack to her head, and a large Mongolian with a gun standing over Jake and Vince.

"I just wanted to send a message that I'm not going to be bullied around," Jake had explained, his gaze on Ben.

After looking over Kimani and getting her an ice pack, Ben hadn't touched or said anything to her. When he'd held her jaw, firm yet gentle, to inspect her injuries, her heart had crumbled. She had wanted his fingers to remain on her forever.

She never got a chance to tell him how awful she felt about the article and to apologize for her part. She wanted to say how sorry she was that she had been so prejudiced at the beginning, so convinced that a guy like him had to be bad. By the time she had realized her error—by the time she had fallen for him—it was too late. Zealous in her mission, she had acted without enough consideration for him or his family.

If she could do it all over again, she would have done things differently.

And now she had created a mess worse than a bull in a china shop.

"So, whatever happened to your rich Asian hottie?" Keisha asked when Kimani went to have her braids undone. They reminded her too much of her time with Ben.

"Back in China," Kimani replied.

After quitting the cabin, Ben had brought everyone except Jake, Vince and Derek onto the jet. She wished she had pulled Ben aside and found the words and the courage. But she had allowed the opportunity to pass, not realizing that she wasn't going to get a chance to speak with him again.

After landing in San Francisco, Ben had had Wong drive Claire and Kimani to the hospital to be checked by a doctor.

"Can you have Ben call me?" Kimani had asked Wong after being dropped off at her home after the hospital. She had handed Wong a slip of paper with her phone number and email.

Three days had passed without word from Ben. She had tried his office and was told by the receptionist that Mr. Lee was in Shanghai, with no return date scheduled.

"He's got to come back to work on his waterfront development," Kimani had said.

"If you need to talk to someone about the development, the project leader is actually Harold Stone, in our office," the receptionist had replied.

Remembering that she had texted and called Sam from Ben's phone, she had gotten his cell number from Sam, but some kind of answering service routed only authorized calls through. Calls originating from unauthorized or blocked phone numbers had to leave a message to be called back.

"You can't write the story," Sam told her as they sat in his office at the *Tribune* offices. "You were in too deep. Especially if you're going to

228

press charges against Jake, you're no longer unbiased."

Expecting that to be Sam's answer, Kimani didn't feel as devastated as she thought she would have been. Her efforts wouldn't be in vain if she could bring someone like Jake to justice and take down the Scarlet Auction. She had told the San Francisco District Attorney all that she knew and had handed over her recording pens so that the D.A.'s office could investigate the Scarlet Auction.

"This is definitely something to look into," the Assistant District Attorney had told Kimani.

It was the bright spot in an otherwise depressing turn of events. At least something positive had come out of it all. Something worth a broken heart.

"I'm not anxious to go back to Trinity County, but I've got to press charges," Kimani said to Sam. "I don't think Claire will."

"That's the woman this Jake strangled till she passed out?"

Kimani nodded. "She said he did it on accident. Apparently he bought a diamond and emerald ring to prove how sorry he was about it."

"A bribe, in other words." Sam shook his head. "I'm sorry about the way things turned out. I should never have let you take this on. It was too dangerous."

"You couldn't have known." Kimani paused.

"You never told me you were going to run an article about Oakland Forward."

"It was a last minute call. Ownership was having a conference call that I just found out about that day."

"The article is not going to be good for Gordon Lee."

"There's nothing in the article that isn't true. If the Lee family didn't do anything wrong, the FPPC investigation will confirm that."

"But meanwhile, they're *suspected* of wrongdoing."

"And maybe they're guilty. We don't know that they aren't."

"They're not guilty."

Sam raised his brows. "How can you be sure? You spent all of three, four days with Benjamin Lee?"

He had a point, Kimani decided, not wanting to be upset with Sam. He was just doing his job.

As if sensing that she was feeling down, Sam said, "Hey, I've got a bit of good news. Even though you can't write the Scarlet Auction expose, I have to hand it to you, it took guts to do what you did. You risked your life."

"Not intentionally," she replied.

"Nonetheless, not all journalists would have put themselves in your place. You stuck your neck out. And I think you would be a great addition to the *Tribune*."

She straightened. "Really?"

He smiled. "Really."

"When?"

"Now."

She let out a shaky breath. "No shit?"

"No shit."

"But what about ownership? How could you be hiring when they're thinking of shutting down the paper?"

"I can't guarantee that your job will last very long, but I can make it work for the time being."

She stamped her feet in glee. Sam got out of his chair to give her a hug.

"Welcome aboard, Kimani Taylor."

Later that night, she celebrated her new job by having margaritas with Keisha and Tara.

"Now all you need is a man," Tara said.

"I got a *job*," Kimani said. "What does that have to do with a man?"

"You can't get it on with a job," Keisha said, as if Kimani should know better.

"My vibrator and I get along just fine."

"You can't convince me it's the same."

"The vibrator can be hella better."

"Un-hunh," Keisha returned in a tone that made Kimani want to throw the tortilla chips at her. "That why you were so mopey the last time we talked about your guy?"

"He wasn't my guy," Kimani emphasized loud and clear, not wanting to remember all the crazy, torturous and amazing things she had experienced at Ben's hands.

"Oh, I know a guy who's free, now that he's dumped that skank of a girlfriend. Marcus. This brother's *fine.*"

Tara nodded and pretended to fan herself.

"He coaches basketball for a junior high school," Keisha added. "You'd have a lot in common. Let me set you up."

"No!"

"Why not? So you can cry over a guy who lives in Hong Kong?"

Kimani blew out a long breath and took a drink of her strawberry margarita. "Fine. But just one date."

"That's all it takes."

Tara raised her glass. "To fine motherfuckin' brothers."

Kimani clinked glasses with Keisha and Tara. Deep down, she knew it was too soon to be dating. She would rather focus on her new job, and she needed time to work Ben out of her system. But it might take a while for that to happen, so maybe it was better to begin the next chapter of her life sooner rather than later.

Tomorrow, she would give Ben one last try. She wasn't expecting to continue anything with him, just the chance to apologize. If he didn't return her call, she could write him an old-fashioned letter to that effect.

After that, she would be ready to close the chapter on being bought, ravaged and tormented by Benjamin Lee.

HIS FOR A WEEK: DEVASTATED
Coming Fall 2018

Made in the USA
Las Vegas, NV
17 April 2021

21621695R00134